GRAVE CONSEQUENCES

SINCLAIR MACLEOD

Published in 2015 by Marplesi

ISBN Paperback: 978-0-9931307-3-1
ISBN eBook: 978-0-9931307-4-8

ALSO AVAILABLE BY SINCLAIR MACLEOD

The Reluctant Detective Series

The Reluctant Detective

The Good Girl

The Killer Performer

The Island Mystery (Short Story)

Russell and Menzies Series

Soulseeker

Inheritance

The Harlequin

DEDICATION

To Andy Millar and Alan Harper, true friends for more years
than any of us would care to admit.

As always, in memory of Calum,
my incredible son and constant inspiration.

ACKNOWLEDGEMENTS

Thanks are due to Emma Hamilton, Geoff Fisher and my patient editor Andy Melvin.

As always my love and thanks also go to Kim, my wife of 27 years and my incredibly wise and gorgeous daughter, Kirsten. I could not write these books without their continued love, support and inspiration.

PROLOGUE

Michelle Armstrong was excited. Judging by his profile, Nick Jackson was exactly what she was looking for. At twenty-nine, he was four years older than she was - a gap she thought ideal. His picture on the dating site showed a fit-looking man with dark hair, an easy, bright smile and green eyes that glinted with a hint of mischief. He had a good career as the owner of a web design company, and seemed to share many of the same interests as she did, including cycling and art. She could not have wished for a more perfect match.

As her high heels clicked and clacked on the paving stones in Royal Exchange Square, a little doubt crept in; maybe Mr Jackson was too good to be true. He probably spent days train spotting, noting numbers in a little black book. Maybe he was just a computer geek or had some other boring hobby that he forgot to mention on his profile. She smiled at the thought and then dismissed it; she had to give him a chance. He had suggested that they should meet in a private club in the city centre, a place where the great and the good of Glaswegian society could congregate to do business and socialise. It was an elegant choice, and showed that Jackson was keen to impress. As she approached the door the first signs of an early autumn shower began to plop large drops of water onto the street. As she stepped into the doorway, Michelle was relieved that the rain would not get the chance to ruin her carefully styled hair.

She walked up the steep stairs to a reception area and told the attractive young woman behind the desk that she was a guest of Mr Jackson. The woman consulted a book that lay open in front of her, and then advised her that Nick Jackson could be found in the main restaurant and gave her the directions to where she would find him.

When she reached the restaurant, a waiter was on duty to escort her to Nick's table. As she approached, Jackson stood and handed her a simple and elegant white rose. She smiled in gratitude as he leaned in and kissed her politely on the cheek, she caught a whiff of expensive and manly cologne, which she found very appealing.

The date was off to a blissful start and she was delighted to see that his photo was an accurate portrait of the athletic, broad-shouldered, handsome man. He held himself with confidence but there was no sign of arrogance. His hair was lustrously thick and she had a sudden urge to run her fingers through it that she managed to resist. One thing his photograph had failed to show was the depth of green that his eyes were, a beautiful colour that reminded her of summer grass.

The waiter handed them both a menu and laid a wine list on the table.

"Can I get you anything to drink while you are choosing your meal and the wine?"

"Can I have a sparkling water, please?" Michelle said.

Jackson thought a moment and said, "I'll have a Peroni, please."

He advised her about the choices on the menu, which may have been condescending when some men did it but Michelle got the sense that he was simply being helpful, so she followed his suggestion and ordered the fish. There was a brief awkward silence as they waited for the waiter to return with their meals. Once the dishes had been delivered they began to chat in the staccato way people do on a first date, but slowly the conversation began to flow more naturally. Nick Jackson was attentive and listened to her stories, asking her for details. He never attempted to hog the conversation but was always willing to answer her questions. During a discussion about art, Nick indicated a belief that Picasso was the greatest artist of all time while Michelle argued for Monet, but they agreed on the genius of Van Gogh. They exchanged stories of family and work, laughing occasionally while sipping on a fragrant Cabernet Sauvignon Blanc that he had ordered to accompany the fish. Michelle was determined to stay relatively sober, so she opted for a coffee rather than a liqueur at the end of the meal while Jackson enjoyed a dram of Jura malt whisky.

When the meal was over, Nick insisted on paying the bill despite Michelle's protestations. She was always wary of letting men pay; for some of them it was as if they were putting a deposit down for something later in the evening, but there was an air about him that assured her that Nick wasn't like that. When the bill had been paid, he offered her a drink in one of the club's bars, but she decided that the evening had been perfect as it was and declined politely. He walked with her through the square under the now starlit night. The rain had stopped, but it had left the pavement shining with the reflections of the atmospheric lighting that illuminated the buildings around the square. Nick offered to walk her back to Buchanan Street Underground Station but as he was heading in the opposite direction, Michelle turned down the offer, insisting there was no need for him to go out of his way and that she would be fine.

As they stood in the shadow of the Duke Of Wellington statue, in front of the Gallery Of Modern Art - a customary traffic cone perched precariously on the Duke's head - Nick said, "I had a great time and I'd really like to see you again."

"Me too. It was a lovely meal and I've really enjoyed being with you."

"I hope you don't expect that kind of dining every time," he replied.

"Oh, I'm used to roughing it, a burger and a coke would be good if I'm with you," she mirrored his grin.

"Can I give you a ring tomorrow and maybe organise a night at the pictures?"

Michelle replied enthusiastically, "That would be lovely, thank you."

"Are you sure I can't walk you to the subway or you could share my cab?"

"No, it's fine it would take you out of your way. You go get your taxi."

"If you're sure."

"I'm sure. Thank you," she said and then stood on her tiptoes as she placed a platonic kiss on his cheek. His smile broadened, they parted with a wave and he walked back along in front of the gallery, going in the direction of the taxi rank on Queen Street.

Michelle began the walk up Queen Street with a beaming smile on her face. Finally, her love life had taken a turn for the better.

She didn't notice that Nick hadn't reached the taxi rank, he had turned back and was now following about fifty yards behind her.

CHAPTER 1

Detective Superintendent Tom Russell lay staring at the ceiling of his bedroom in the unseasonably and uncomfortably warm late-September morning. According to his alarm clock it was five forty-five on a Saturday. His insomnia was now a persistent fact of life, a regular restless tussle with a conscience that refused to let him rest. It was now a year and five months since the man who called himself the Harlequin had murdered Russell's ex-wife. Karen's face haunted him; not the smiling, carefree woman he had married; nor the doubtful scowl that darkened her face during her bouts of jealousy; not even the look of disdain that she cast at him on the day they were divorced. The face he saw every night - and even at times during the day - was the frozen, distant, unseeing gaze that had gripped her at the moment of her death; the horrible pale blue cast to her skin; her soulless face, and hair infused with ice crystals like some hellish vision of the Snow Queen.

His only attempt to combat the nightmarish wraith had come in a frequent and dangerous contest with bottles of whisky. Some nights he would sit with the golden liquid in front of him on his small dining table, staring at it as it dared him to drink and forget. Occasionally it would find its way into a glass and he would inhale the peaty smell before pouring it back into the bottle. On most nights he won the battle, but with increasing regularity - particularly at the weekends - the whisky was gaining a foothold in his life. Half a bottle could disappear in an hour before he made his way to bed. The soporific effect of the alcohol was normally enough to send him off to sleep, but it wouldn't prevent him waking up in the early hours of the morning, sweat dripping from every pore, with that same ghostly face floating through his mind.

She was there again this morning and after half an hour of tossing and turning, Russell gave up trying to get back to sleep. He slouched along the short hall of his flat to the kitchen, where he switched on the kettle and put a tea bag into a mug.

When the drink was ready, he moved through to the living room, and glanced at the wedding photo that now adorned his sideboard. He had retrieved it from the depths of a box at the back of the hall cupboard, in an attempt to replace the image of Karen's lifelessness with that of her smiling in happier times. It hadn't worked, and he knew it was increasingly unlikely that it would ever drive the guilt and grief from his mind.

In the wake of Karen's murder he had been forced to take some leave from work. His boss - believing he was helping him - had instructed him to attend the force psychologist, but Russell's inability to articulate his emotions combined with a professional who seemed reluctant to delve too deeply and was simply happy to tick boxes, meant that he had returned to work before he had truly addressed the maelstrom of his complicated feelings. Since then the once dedicated detective found himself going through the mechanics of the job with no real engagement on his part; an automaton running through its programming.

When the anniversary of Karen's death came around, his sense of detachment became desperation. He paid cursory visits to crime scenes and let his colleague - DI Alex Menzies - lead the majority of investigations. Officially, this was how a detective superintendent was supposed to act, but Russell had always been given more leeway than most, due to his skills as both a manager and a detective. The change to his personality had turned him into the very thing that he used to hate - an administrator. He became simply a conduit between the Procurator Fiscal's Office or the senior management team, and the officers of the Major Incident Team. As he sat in his flat with his tea, he was once again wondering if it was time to end his career as a police officer.

*

Tommy Renwick wasn't keen on working on a Saturday morning (he couldn't have a wee drink on a Friday night) but there was nothing else for it; if it was your shift, it was your shift. The grounds of the city's most famous cemetery were relatively easy to maintain, but with the first fall of autumn leaves Tommy and his colleagues were a little busier.

The monumental sculptures of Glasgow Necropolis were an incredible collection of funereal art. There were angels; crosses; solemn figures and elaborate tombs that all combined to produce a magnificent city of the dead; a vision of heaven on earth. Time had taken its toll on some parts of the old place, some statues now stood headless and heedless; the carving on some stones weathered to illegibility by wind and rain; ivy grew from cracks as new life claimed the ground, nature's victory over death. Casual vandalism had turned some of the tombs into garish splashes of exuberant colour amongst the otherwise sombre Presbyterian greys and browns of the majority of the monuments. There were obelisks pointing the way to heaven - just in case the dead needed directions to their final destination - as well as strange stone urns draped in petrified cloth; death hidden from prying eyes. The grand mausoleums were as much a tribute to the ego of the architects as they were acknowledgements of the achievements of the deceased, but even they were crumbling at the edges as entropy proved that even death wasn't the end. The Necropolis - like much of the living city - was a place of fading, Victorian grandeur.

Tommy loved the old place like it was his own garden. The expanse of the mossy grounds that were normally relatively quiet meant he didn't need to talk to people too often. He didn't have much time for the living with their petty concerns, selfishness and trivial problems; the city of the dead was the perfect place for him. The residents never said anything stupid or ever let you down. He loved working among the sculptures and graves, reading the names and creating stories in his imagination from the inscriptions. He composed tales of families losing children, great men reduced by circumstance as business went bust, wives cheated and cheating. He thought he could write a book from those inscriptions.

He was driving around in his little electric maintenance cart when he spotted someone lying up against one of the gravestones. Every so often he would find a drunk or junkie taking shelter in the protection of the monuments. It always irked him that they had so little respect for the dead or the beauty of the cemetery, and he for one wasn't going to tolerate it.

"Hey, you. Get aff o' there," he shouted in the direction of the prone figure. There was no response and Renwick continued to shout admonishments as he approached. The closer he got, the stranger the figure appeared and the more doubt crept into his voice. He was a very superstitious man and the sight of a woman in a full ivory-coloured Victorian wedding dress brought thoughts of a ghost, the soul of a lady raised from the grave, back to haunt him. Reluctantly, he stopped the cart and edged his way towards the woman. When he was standing over her, he could see that she was no ghost, but even to Tommy's untrained eye it was clear from the grey paleness of her skin that she was dead. He crossed himself as he backed away as if scared she was going to stand up and reach for him. When he bumped into his cart, he turned and climbed into it. He drove about a hundred yards from the body and dialled 999 on his mobile phone.

*

On a clear day the peak of the Glasgow Necropolis hill offered great views across the city, but not if you were standing in a forensics tent. Although it protected the evidence of a murder from the vagaries of the elements, it hardly counted as scenic.

Alex Menzies found herself staring at the wall of the tent rather than the view she would normally have of Glasgow

Cathedral and beyond. When she looked down she saw the incongruous site of a woman's body, laid out with a mortician's skill, her arms across her chest. Her hair had been combed and arrayed with careful attention. She looked slightly misshapen due to the way that the silk of the dress had settled over her body. Her eyes were closed and there was a sense that she had been treated very respectfully. Despite the care, the chances were that the person who had laid her out had first taken her life. It was a distinctly odd crime scene.

The detective inspector had been called out an hour earlier by an incredulous detective sergeant from London Road police station. He had sounded concerned that Alex would dismiss him as some kind of raving lunatic when he told her that a 'Victorian' woman had been found in the grand old cemetery. She had listened patiently, surprised but she assured him that she would be there as soon as she could.

The forensic team had arrived only two minutes behind her, and immediately began to process the scene by covering the body and the immediate area with the tent. An outer perimeter had been established by closing the graveyard to visitors, while taping off an area fifty yards from the body in every direction created the inner cordon.

Sean O'Reilly was standing in the tent with Alex. The strange sight perplexed him equally. "You ever seen anythin' like this before, Alex?" he asked in his broad Dublin accent.

"No. You?"

"Not at all. It's bloody weird."

"Has the pathologist been called?"

"Yes, it's Dr McNeill who's on-call. She's on her way. Are you goin' to call Tom?"

"I'm not sure, Sean. It's getting difficult to know how to deal with him, he's so remote and disinterested these days." It had been bothering her for some time and now she felt she had to tell someone. "I think he's going to resign."

"Really? That's not good. Although he has been through a lot, I can understand why he would want to quit."

"You're right but it doesn't make him any easier to work with. One part of me wants the old boss back; the other just wants him to go now if he's planning to go. It wouldn't be great for the team but it might be better for him. Spending time with him at the moment is one long grind."

O'Reilly paused before he said, "You should ring him. It's his choice whether to come or not."

"I know, I need to follow procedure, it's up to him whether he wants to do the same."

She stepped out of the tent; she struggled for a few seconds as she tried to get to her pocket through the paper forensics suit she was wearing, before finally pulling her mobile phone out. She removed the blue latex gloves that covered her hands and tapped on Russell's name in her contacts list. The phone rang four times before he answered.

"Alex?"

"Good morning, sir."

"What's up?" She could tell by his tone he was less than delighted to hear from her.

"We've got a body in Glasgow Necropolis."

"If I'm not mistaken, Detective Inspector, there are thousands of bodies in the Necropolis," he replied sarcastically.

She managed to bite her tongue and she gave him a censored version of the answer his response deserved. "This one's a little fresher than those that are buried here."

"Give me the details."

Alex told him what they knew, which at that moment wasn't much.

"Are you sure she's one of ours? She hasn't just been on the piss at some fancy dress party and died during the night, of hypothermia or something?"

"Not unless she laid herself out in preparation for death. She's been staged by someone, lying there as if she's in a coffin, hair combed and make-up perfect."

He sighed with resignation. "Right, I'll be there as soon as I can."

Alex ended the call and then let her own long sigh escape into the air. Her respect for the abilities of her boss as a detective and manager remained undiminished, but her admiration for him as a person was waning fast.

A short time later, Dr McNeill arrived and suited up. In the three months since she had returned from maternity leave, every time Alex had met the doctor she had looked exhausted. Her baby boy was now nearly a year old but he still wasn't sleeping well. Combining her role as a forensic pathologist with that of being a mother was proving to be taxing for the likeable Hebridean islander.

"Good morning, Alex," she said when she was ready.

"Good morning, Doctor. How is Ruaridh?"

"Still gorgeous, still blethering in a language all of his creation and laughing at three o'clock in the morning," she replied with a weary smile.

"At least he's laughing," Alex responded.

"What have you got for me today?"

"It's certainly different, I doubt you will have seen anything quite like it. We've got a young woman in her early to mid-twenties, there's no sign of any obvious trauma, and she's wearing an antique wedding dress."

"Curious. Let's have a look then shall we?"

As the pathologist lifted the flap of the tent, Noel Hawthorn pulled up in his battered Mercedes at the edge of the blue and white tape. Noel was a Londoner, who was both the crime scene photographer and Alex's boyfriend. He lifted his camera bag from the boot of the car, dressed for the scene and then ducked under the tape.

"Good morning, you" he beamed at Alex in the way she loved. His striking face always seemed even more handsome when he looked at her that way.

Their relationship was in a bit of a limbo as Alex was finding it difficult to move beyond the stage they were currently at. She didn't want any deeper commitment than the nights out; the overnight stays at each other's flats, and the intense and loving sex they enjoyed. She knew that it was stupid to still have trust issues nearly three years after she had thrown out her former fiancé for bedding at least one other woman. Noel was keen to see things progress and asked her a couple of times if she wanted to move in with him, but she had resisted. He said that it was fine and that he would wait until she was ready, but she felt that she was in danger of straining their relationship. Did she love him? She thought so, but the issue of her lack of faith in any man was one that she could not reconcile so that she could move on.

They had agreed that although all their colleagues knew of their relationship, there would be no gestures of affection between them while they were working, so Alex just returned Noel's infectious grin and said, "Good morning yourself."

"What delights have we got today? Is it a chibbing, a gubbing or maybe a malkying?"

She laughed at his attempt to speak in the Glaswegian vernacular. His London roots all too obvious in his dreadful effort. She told him about the body and his face reflected his surprise and curiosity.

"Not your standard Friday night Glaswegian murder then."

"Definitely not."

"Are they ready for me?"

"Dr McNeill's just gone in."

"I better get started."

Alex decided to leave the forensic experts to get on with their job of collating the initial evidence of the strange crime. She moved away from the tent and looked out over the city. The smell of autumn was in the air, a slight tang of musty decay. It was a warm day; the sun was trying to shine through a low blanket of hazy cloud. Where it managed to alight on the stones it gave the graves a daub of colour as it emphasised the lichen and moss. The view was restricted due to the roiling patches of mist, but she could still see the Gothic cathedral and the expanse of the Royal Infirmary. Although the cemetery was about one hundred and seventy-years old it was relatively new compared to the buildings that neighboured it; this part of the city was where it's roots were firmly planted. The cathedral had stood since 1197 and Provand's Lordship, the oldest house in the city which was built in the 15th century, and was a stone's throw from the cathedral. The Necropolis had absorbed that history in a way that made it feel even more ancient than it was. As if the monuments had been laid down in pre-Christian times, like the standing stones and burial cairns that could be found all across Scotland.

This was a cemetery for the elite of Victorian society. The gravestones and great statues marked the final resting place of architects; doctors; ministers, lawyers; politicians; writers and merchants, interned with their families in plots, which varied in size according to their position in society. Alex knew there was another graveyard close by where there was no acknowledgement of those who were laid to rest, the poor and unknown, a Potter's field. She reflected that death may be the great leveller but even after they were gone, those with wealth and those in poverty were differentiated by places like this.

From her vantage point, she could see the crime-scene manager organising a team of uniformed officers who were about to begin a painstaking search of the expanse of the graves. As well as scanning the ground for possible physical evidence, they would have to check each and every tomb to see if any of them had been used as a host for the murderous events of the previous night. She didn't envy them their task and was glad that those days were well behind her.

She had been watching the search for about fifteen minutes when she heard her name being called. She turned to see Jacqui Kerr, the Procurator Fiscal responsible for prosecuting murder in the city. In Scotland, the police work on behalf of the Fiscal's office and Ms Kerr made sure that every detective and officer knew it. Like everyone else, Alex had a professional but cool relationship with the acerbic woman.

She walked back to the tent.

"Detective Menzies."

"Good morning," Alex replied pointedly, angered by the woman's curt lack of manners.

"Where's your boss?"

"On his way."

"I'm not pleased with his attitude lately." It was indicative of Kerr's style that there was little in the way of tact in how she spoke to people. Her abrupt demeanour and perceived lack of ability made her an ill-liked figure among the personnel of the city's police stations.

Despite her difficulties with Russell, Alex felt a need to defend him. "He's been through a lot and he's still trying to come to terms with what happened."

"It was his *ex*-wife and it's well over a year ago. I would have thought he would be over it by now."

Alex's ire increased at the other woman's high-handed attitude. "She may have been his ex-wife but he did love her once. He also feels guilty about our inability to catch Dent before we did."

Kerr seemed immune to Alex's response. "Well, he only has himself to blame as far as that goes."

The detective found herself clenching her teeth in an attempt to stop her saying something she would regret. She took a breath and said, "Shall we go in?"

"Wouldn't you rather wait for Superintendent Russell?"

"He'll be here soon enough," Alex snapped.

The Fiscal acquiesced and Alex led her into the tent that was beginning to feel a little cramped. Dr McNeill was still taking notes and recording everything that may or not be relevant to the woman's death. Occasionally, she would ask Noel to capture a specific angle that may prove vital in discovering how the victim died or who her killer may be. Sean O'Reilly was bagging and cataloguing trace evidence.

Ten minutes after Alex and the Fiscal had walked into the tent, it became even more crowded when Russell arrived. Dressed in a white protective suit with the hood pulled up, nothing except his face was visible but when Alex looked into his red-ringed eyes she could see that he was once again far from his best.

"You decided to honour us with your presence," Kerr observed.

"Well spotted Jacqui. I can see why you rose to the dizzy heights of the legal profession. It must be your razor-sharp intellect and observational skills that did it." His voice sounded rough and his tone was combative.

Russell's already strained working relationship with the Fiscal had deteriorated rapidly in the last few months. When possible, he would communicate with her by e-mail but when they did speak it was with a deep sense of mutual loathing.

An indignant Kerr said, "You walk a very thin line, Detective Superintendent."

Russell ignored her. "What's the story, Doctor McNeill?"

"Good morning, Superintendent. I'm afraid there's not a lot I can tell you. There is no obvious sign of either blunt force or sharp force trauma, no strangulation or suffocation, so I can't tell you for sure how she was killed. She's probably been re-dressed, so I'll learn a lot more once we remove the costume."

"So this might not even be murder?" he asked with disgust.

"Possibly, but I would be surprised if it was natural causes," she replied without any sign of annoyance at his attitude.

Russell turned to his DI and asked, "Who found her?"

"The cemetery attendant, at about nine this morning."

"When do the gates open?"

"He opened up at seven-thirty but he was working the other side of the hill for the first part of his shift, so he didn't see who left her here or any vehicle."

"I presume that he had checked the place last night."

"He said he was past this grave about midday yesterday."

"Doc, what's the time of death?"

"Judging by liver temperature, she died in the early hours of this morning."

"So she has been moved from where she was killed if her body was left here some time this morning between half-past seven and nine," Russell said, voicing his own thoughts rather than to inform anyone in the tent.

"Any identification?"

Sean O'Reilly answered, "No, she had no handbag or phone. It was just the body."

"Will you be able to do the PM today, Doctor McNeill?"

"I'll need to check with the mortuary but we'll need an identification before we can do anything."

"Of course, sorry. We'll need to get on that, Alex."

'Yes, sir. Where do you want to run the investigation from?"

As they were between two large stations, Russell took his time while he considered his options and decided on London Road.

"I'll leave you to it. First priority is an ID." Russell left the tent and Alex followed him.

Tommy Renwick was sitting on his cart just outside the cemetery gates, obviously shaken by what had happened. Alex spent a few minutes with him, reassuring him and gently probing him for information but there was nothing more he could remember that was relevant. His encounter with the corpse had left him numb and he was still trying to process what had happened. Alex organised a cup of sweet tea for him and left him her card before she followed Russell to London Road station.

CHAPTER 2

She arrived at London Road about twenty minutes after her boss, where he was waiting impatiently at the front desk. The station is a relatively modern, dull grey building that was once the HQ of the old 'E' division. Since the Strathclyde force had been absorbed into the new Police Scotland organisation it was now the main station responsible for the east side of the city.

The officer in charge was Superintendent Catriona Carmichael. She was around the same age as Russell, and they had worked together at various points over the previous twenty years. It had been a while since they had seen each other, so when Russell and Menzies made their way to her office, Superintendent Carmichael greeted Russell with a beaming smile.

"Tom, good to see you." She stepped from behind her desk and wrapped a surprised Russell in a warm embrace.

Alex studied the woman who she knew by reputation was a good copper. She was tall and busty with a strong, but attractive face. She wore her age well; her hair styled in a modern way, a minimal touch of make-up, her skin clear and radiant, it all combined to help her look younger than her near fifty years. She was known as a strong, intelligent boss with a flair for organisation and team building. She had spent two years at the police training college in Tulliallan as an instructor before she had returned to operational duty as the senior officer at London Road.

Russell recovered from his embarrassment and said, "It's good to see you too Catriona. Have you met my DI, Alex Menzies?"

"Alex, a pleasure. I've heard a lot of good things about you."

"Thanks, likewise." Alex replied, feeling slightly self-conscious but nowhere near as much as her boss appeared to be. He wasn't the most effusive or tactile person, but Carmichael had broken through his barriers in a way Alex had never seen anyone else do.

The superintendent sat down and invited her visitors to do the same. "Tom, I was so sorry to hear about Karen."

"I got your card, thanks. How's Bill?" he replied, moving the subject of the conversation on as quickly as he could.

"He's fine, but we're not together any more, our divorce should be through in a couple of weeks."

"I'm sorry to hear that."

"You know what this job's like, Tom. It doesn't always leave you time for the things you should be concentrating on. Bill and I just drifted apart; it's better for both of us if we move on. He's already found someone new, and I say good luck to him. He's a decent man and he deserves to be happy. So what brings MIT to my neck of the woods?"

Russell replied, "We're going to have to set up an incident room here if you can squeeze us in."

"The body in the Necropolis."

"Aye, it looks like murder and it was a toss up between here and Stewart Street, so I thought I'd come and see an old friend."

Alex was both surprised and delighted to see a glimmer of the old Tom Russell appear, however briefly. She felt she was constantly monitoring his mood, trying to judge how he would react in certain situations. It was exhausting but at least Superintendent Carmichael had lifted him a little bit from his sullen dourness.

"What's the story?"

Russell recanted what little they knew of the bridal corpse.

"Very peculiar. I'm sure we can squeeze you in," the superintendent replied warmly. "I'll get our administrator to find you a room."

"Thanks Catriona. I'll keep you informed of our progress. Hopefully, we'll not be in your hair for too long."

"Take as long as you need and if I can find a way to help you with the overtime budget, let me know. I'm pretty sure the bosses and politicians will be keen to have this cleared up quickly and I'm a pretty good negotiator with the brass."

"Yes, they're going to be a little uneasy and probably a huge pain in my arse."

"You know where I am if you need some support."

"Thanks again."

Carmichael made a quick phone call to the civilian administrator, who arrived to lead them to an office that was already equipped with computers and phones.

Russell left Alex to begin the process of assembling the team while he went to a local mobile snack bar for some breakfast.

*

The identification of the victim proved to be a much easier task than they initially thought it was going to be. Janet Kerry had called the police station in Partick when her flatmate had failed to come home the previous night. The desk sergeant had immediately circulated the details to other stations and from that description a connection was made to the woman in the cemetery. Michelle Armstrong's perfect night had ended in tragedy.

When the information was brought to the attention of Russell and Menzies, Tom Russell instructed Alex to begin the investigation in earnest by interviewing Janet Kerry.

Alex rang DS Ann-Marie Craigan, who was now seconded to the Major Incident Team. The woman from Northern Ireland had impressed Russell during previous investigations, and when one of the permanent members of the team had gone off on long-term sick leave, Russell had requested Craigan be assigned as cover. Although it didn't offer a promotion, Craigan had jumped at the opportunity to join them as it gave her a chance to enhance her experience and her CV.

After supplying her with the address, Alex told the DS to meet her at the flat Janet Kerry had shared with the victim.

Ms Kerry was a fleshy woman in her mid-twenties. Her green eyes were already cloaked in concern when she opened the door to the two detectives who were displaying their warrant cards. She dropped her head as if scared to even look at them.

"Ms Kerry, can we come in, please?" Alex asked.

"Sorry, yes. Something's happened to Michelle, hasn't it?" The small light of hope she had for her friend was dimming rapidly as a result of a knock on her door. Both officers were used to seeing that candle extinguished in many eyes when they arrived in someone's life.

"It's better if we talk inside the house," Alex said softly.

The now nervous woman moved through to the living room with her unwanted visitors at her back. The room was bright and modern, with simple dark-wood furniture and a collection of small items that stamped the character of the two women on their home. Janet sank into a chair while the other two detectives settled into a black leather sofa.

"You reported Ms Armstrong missing earlier today, do you have a photograph of her?" Alex asked.

From an occasional table at the side of her chair Kerry lifted her mobile phone, tapped the screen and then flicked a few times before handing the device to the detective.

Alex looked down at the picture and into a familiar face, the face of the woman in the cemetery. She passed the phone back.

As gently as she could she said, "I'm sorry to tell you that a body we believe to be Ms Armstrong's was found early this morning."

Kerry gasped, "Oh, no." The distraught friend wept quietly for a short while, the detectives were caught in the awkward chasm of grief as they had been many times before.

Ann-Marie Craigan said, "I'll make a cup of tea."

"Thanks," Alex replied, glad that the spell of silence had been broken. She watched as Janet Kerry continued to cry, slowly composing herself and by the time the tea had been served she was ready to talk.

Alex was sensitive to Janet Kerry's plight but the necessary questions of the investigation had to begin. "Can you tell us where Michelle was last night?"

"She went out on a date. I told her not to go, I said that it was too dodgy using that bloody website." It was unclear to whom the bitterness she felt was directed.

"This is a dating website?"

"Yes, it's called 'caledonialove.com', it claims to be an elite site for Scottish professionals. At least that's what Michelle told me. But I said to her, I told her that anybody could post any old shite up there, it wouldn't make it true."

"Was it a man she was going to meet?"

"Yes."

"Do you know his name?"

"She didn't tell me but you should be able to find it somewhere on her laptop. You'll need to take it with you, won't you?"

"Yes, we will. It's important that we start the investigation as quickly as possible; it will give us the best chance to catch whoever did this. You will get it back if you need it."

"That's fine. I'd like it back, there are lots of photos on there that I would like to keep."

"You and Ms Armstrong were flatmates but was there more to your relationship?"

"We ran a café together just off Sauchiehall Street. It's called Cuppa Joe. We set it up about nine months ago. It's just a breakfast and lunch place but it's become quite popular. I suppose I might have to close it now." Alex could see that the woman felt her life was collapsing in on her.

"Did you ever have anyone come in to the café that took an unhealthy interest in Ms Armstrong?"

Janet looked puzzled. "What do you mean?"

"Maybe a man who made inappropriate comments to her, or asked her out and she refused."

"Like a stalker?"

"Not necessarily just someone who seemed interested in a way that was out of the ordinary."

She thought for a short time. "No, not that I know of anyway. There are a few of the guys who like her. She is the kind of woman that most men find attractive." She realised the she had used the wrong tense. "*Was* the kind of woman."

"Do you have a printed photograph we could have of Ms Armstrong?"

"One moment." She was gone for a couple of minutes and when she returned she was clutching a picture of her with Michelle. They both looked tired but happy. "This was at the launch of Cuppa Joe. Is it recent enough?"

"I'm sure it will be fine. I'm sorry about this but we'll need someone to make a formal identification. Would that be you?"

"I could but it should probably be her family. Do you want me to tell them? I'd rather not, if you don't mind."

Alex shook her head. "No, don't you worry about that, we'll take care of it. If you give us their address, we'll send someone to speak to them."

"Thanks, I don't think I could have handled that." She reached for her phone once more and supplied the information Alex needed.

"I'm sorry for your loss, Ms Kerry. If there's anything you need or if you remember anything that might be relevant, please give me a call." She handed over her card and then Kerry went to Michelle's bedroom to get the laptop.

While she was gone Alex asked Craigan, "What do you think?"

"The dating thing?" she responded in the harsh cadence of her Belfast accent.

Alex nodded.

"Sounds like a good starting point."

"Maybe the guy wasn't pleased that he didn't get what he wanted from her last night."

"A good chance but what's with the period costume stuff?"

"Fetish? Who knows but we'll have to take a good look at this 'elite professional'."

Kerry returned with the laptop in a protective sleeve.

"Thanks for this, we'll get it back to you as soon as we can." Alex said.

"I told her but she wouldn't listen," were her parting words as she closed the door. Janet Kerry had started to blame herself, there was no point in Alex telling her that it wasn't her fault, she would come to that conclusion herself, even though it would probably be quite some time away and there would be many dark days in between.

CHAPTER 3

Alex asked Ann-Marie Craigan to take on the task of telling Michelle Armstrong's parents of their daughter's death. She then called to arrange a Family Liaison Officer be allocated to the victim's family, and suggested that the officer meet Craigan at the Armstrong house in Knightswood. She knew that she could trust the detective sergeant to handle the onerous task with empathy and tact. The questions that needed to be asked about their daughter's life, friends and acquaintances would have to wait for another time. Craigan would also accompany the Armstrongs to the mortuary for the official identification of the young woman's body. Only then could formal proceedings really begin.

When Alex had finished her list of administrative duties, she called Russell.

"Yes?" he snapped.

"The woman's name is Michelle Armstrong. She was on a date last night that was arranged through a dating website. I've got her laptop and I'm going to drive out to Gartcosh to see if the IT genies can help us work out who she was meeting."

"That's fine. Keep me informed."

Once again the call ended abruptly and Alex's already thin patience was stretched a little bit further. If he continued to be so distant and downright rude, she didn't know how much longer she could work with him.

*

She drove to the brand new Scottish Crime Campus, which is home to a number of departments that deal with serious crime across the country. The forensics teamed share the building with the Scottish Serious Organised Crime Task Force; members of the specialist crime division; the Crown Office, staff from the Procurator Fiscal's office, the National Crime Agency and HMRC.

Due to the nature of the sensitive work that was undertaken in the building, the security procedures were very stringent. Alex's identification was checked thoroughly, she had to walk through an airport-style metal detector and the bag with the laptop was inspected carefully before she was guided to the IT office by a humourless and uncommunicative security guard.

Roger Green was always happy to see Alex. The middle-aged Senior Forensic IT Technician had worked with her on many occasions and they had a friendly, at times flirtatious working relationship. He and his team were now an integral part of the investigative arsenal of the police and Alex relied on them as much as any of the officers on the street. She liked the genial big man and she knew that he was among the best at what he did.

This was her first visit since the team had moved into the facility earlier in the year, but it looked like they had occupied the space for years. Everywhere she looked every surface seemed to be covered in pieces of technology in various states of repair. Each was labelled or bagged according to the case they were associated with. Alex had no idea how they could keep track of everything but she knew that their procedures were as stringent as every other department involved in the chain of evidence.

Green looked delighted when he saw the detective bearing another piece of hardware that needed his expertise.

His Somerset accent was evident when he said, "DI Menzies, what brings you to our new dungeon?"

"Another wee puzzle, Roger. One I'm sure you'll sail through in minutes."

"You flatter me, but it'll get you everywhere." Roger's flirtations were always gentle and Alex never took offence at them. Roger had been married for thirty years and was dedicated to his wife; on one visit he had spent the time telling Alex all about how they had met and a good bit of their life together. The easy chat was all part of the banter that they enjoyed to help get them through the day.

Alex handed him the laptop case while explaining the background to what she needed him to do.

"Let's have a look."

He removed the computer from its bag and placed it on his desk where there were multiple mobile phones and three desktop computers stacked on top of each other each bearing a label stuck to the back. He pushed the phones to one side and created enough space to get to work on Michelle

Armstrong's digital life. He connected the power cable and started up the machine.

"Do you think the details of the date she was on will be in her e-mail account? Alex asked.

"No, these sites tend to keep the member's e-mail addresses private, just in case on of their clients is a creepy stalker. They have their own messaging system."

When the power up sequence was completed he said, "No password. She wasn't very security conscious."

Green loaded the web browser and began typing the site address. When the login screen appeared he said, "We're in luck, the machine has cached her login details."

Alex watched while Michelle Armstrong's profile appeared. The site's logo was a stylised version of two intertwined this-tles, and Michelle's photograph appeared beside it at the top of the page. There were four tabs coloured to match the thistle theme, entitled Me; Matches; Messages; and My Account.

Roger clicked on the 'Messages' tab. It didn't take long to find the details of Michelle's meeting with Nick Jackson.

"You didn't need my genius this time Alex, you could have done this yourself," Green observed.

"I wouldn't bet on that," she said graciously. "I'm grateful, Roger. Now I need to go and find out a little more about Mr Jackson."

Green shut down the computer and packed it away before handing the case back to Alex.

"That's just a small favour you me this time," he said.

"Roger, my debt keeps rising, someday I'll take you for a pint, honest."

He laughed and waved as she left him to his collection of phones that may or may not help to put some drug dealers in jail.

*

The office at London Road station had already taken on the characteristics of a major incident room. Michelle Armstrong's photograph had been posted on a large whiteboard with the brief details of who she was. The beginnings of a timeline had been drawn at the bottom of the board indicating the time of her date, when the park opened, the time her body was found, and a shaded area indicating Dr McNeill's estimated time of death.

Half the desks were occupied by detectives and uniformed officers who were undertaking the collation of information. Alex nodded to those who looked up from their work while she walked to the desk in the corner where Russell had taken up temporary residence. The life of the senior investigating officers in a difficult murder investigation was an itinerant one, and the two detectives were used to setting up their base in a variety of stations across Glasgow and beyond. Russell had once referred to them as the alternative NHS, the Nomadic Homicide Squad.

When he noticed the DI approaching, he put down his pen, removed his glasses - a recent addition that he now had to wear for reading and working with the computer - and turned his chair towards her.

"So, what have you got?"

"Michelle was out last night with a guy called Nick Jackson."

"What do we know about him?"

"Let's have a look." Alex went through the same process that Green had previously, until it brought her to the screen where she could click on the link to Jackson's profile.

She began to read the details for the benefit of the other detectives who Russell had instructed to listen. She listed his age, career and interests.

"No address I suppose?" Russell asked.

"No, but there is a mobile number for him."

"That's a start, but if he's our man, I doubt he's going to come running if we ring him, do you?" Russell sounded tired, irritable and a little bitter, as if he just wanted the case to be over with as little effort as possible.

Alex took the lead. "We can ask the Fiscal to arrange a warrant for the records of the dating agency. According to the website it's registered in Stirling."

"Sir, could we ask the telecoms people to help out?" a rookie DC asked.

"We'd still need a warrant, Constable. Or did you miss that training session at Tulliallan," Russell barked to the embarrassment of the young detective.

Alex offered a kinder reply. "They could but we'd need to know which company he was with to make the warrant specific enough. We'll go down that track if we need to, but personally I think it's worth just asking the dating agency if they'll help."

Russell sighed. "It might be worth a try but I'm pretty sure you'll get the client confidentiality bollocks as an answer. We'll still need the warrant, but in the meantime it might be worth a visit to the restaurant. If he's a member there, they'll have his details on file."

To help the young detective recover some confidence Alex said, "DC…?"

"Hendry, ma'am."

"DC Hendry would you give the agency a ring and see if they'll co-operate."

"Yes ma'am," he said eagerly, glad to feel useful rather than like a complete pillock. He'd heard a lot about Russell and had been looking forward to working with him, the detective superintendent was renowned as a decent boss but if that was decent, he hated to think what a bastard would be like.

"Are you coming to the club?" Alex asked.

"No, you go. I've already had ACC Posh Twat on moaning about the effects on tourism if this drags on. Fuckin' arsehole. He wants a written progress report every day, probably to make sure his shiny arse is covered. It's terribly inconvenient that lassie getting herself murdered and messing up his stats."

Exhausted by his rancorous negativity, Alex set off for the city centre.

CHAPTER 4

The sophisticated decor of the club where Nick Jackson and Michelle Armstrong had dined looked a little different in the light of a late summer's day; more attuned to the needs of business meetings rather than amorous encounters.

Alex had shown her warrant card at the desk where the receptionist called the manager and told her that there was a detective to see her. The woman who arrived was in her early thirties, immaculately attired in a black business suit, with a knee-length skirt and a short, well-tailored jacket. Underneath the jacket was a pearl-coloured silk blouse that looked expensive, and around her neck a circular jade stone hung from a designer necklace. Alex felt quite underdressed in her simple light blue blouse and trousers. The manager's heavy make-up did a fine job of disguising her age but Alex thought that she might be in her early forties.

She smiled in a practiced way with as much sincerity as she could fake and said, "I'm Kara Smith. How can I help you, Detective…?"

"Detective Inspector Alex Menzies. Can we go somewhere a bit more private?"

Her simulated smile cracked a little as she replied, "This sounds serious."

"It is."

Alex was led through a network of corridors and up three flights of stairs to the manager's office, which was situated at the top of the building.

"It's quite a place you have here," Alex observed when they were both seated.

"Three restaurants serving a variety of cuisine, four bars and two function rooms. It keeps me busy." It sounded like the script she had learned and trotted out repeatedly to prospective members. "Can I get you a mineral water or something else to drink?"

"No, thank you."

"How can I help you?"

Alex felt an irrational irritation at the woman. She had only just met her but there was an air of falseness about her that went far beyond the obviously dyed hair and surgically enhanced breasts. The detective struggled to keep the illogical annoyance out of her voice as she said, "A young woman was here for dinner last night with one of your members, that young woman is now dead. We believe she may have been murdered and we'd like to talk to her companion. His name is Nick Jackson."

Ms Smith looked like someone had prodded her with a Taser. "Surely not. Our membership is very exclusive," she said haughtily.

Alex knew from the glossy leaflet she had read while waiting for the manager, that the prices were not prohibitive and she doubted that there would be too much vetting of the clientele. Custom was money after all. She knew from a report that had crossed her desk that at least one gangland figure had had a birthday party in the club's function room but she let the comment pass.

"I'm not saying the gentleman is responsible, I'm simply saying that as one of the last people to see her alive, he may have information that will be helpful to the investigation."

Some of the manager's initial shock and outrage dissipated and she acknowledged, "Oh, yes I see."

"Ideally, we'd like his home address so that we can interview him and rule him out of our enquiries."

"I'm sorry but it's not company policy to give out the details of our clients."

Alex imagined DC Hendry hearing a very similar speech from someone at the dating agency. She used a tired line that she had used often in the past. "We can get a warrant."

"I'm afraid that's what you'll have to do," Smith said defensively.

"And I suppose the same goes for your security footage?"

"Of course. The privacy of our guests is our highest priority." The defensiveness was replaced with an indignant defiance.

"Ms Smith, when was the last time you were visited by inspectors from Environmental Health or the HMRC?" Alex asked casually.

Smith did not rise to the threat. "You can try to blackmail me all you want Inspector, but don't think for a minute I'm going to bow to your bullying."

Worth a try, thought Alex.

"We'll just have to contact the Fiscal's office."

"You do just that. I'll show you out."

"One more thing. I'd like to speak to the person who served the couple last night."

"I suppose that would be appropriate. Follow me."

Smith led Alex out of her office and down the dull beige service stairwell to the kitchen area. The kitchen was bustling with sous chefs preparing vegetables for the day's diners. Amongst the industrious activity Smith spoke to a middle-aged man, dressed formally in a suit with a silk waistcoat, shirt and tie. Alex guessed that he was the Maître D'. After a short consultation he disappeared into another room. He returned with a younger man whose tie was loose, his waistcoat was unbuttoned and he looked nowhere near as dapper as the older man. When Smith saw him she barked, "Smarten yourself up Gaughan."

"I was on a break." The younger man responded before tightening his tie, straightening his collar and fastening his waistcoat.

"Inspector Menzies this is Roddy Gaughan. Mr Gaughan, this is Detective Inspector Menzies. She would like to talk to you about a couple of guests that you attended to last night."

"Right, No problem."

"I'll leave you to it," Smith said before marching away.

"Do you mind if I have a smoke while we're talking?" Gaughan asked Alex.

"Sure, it won't take long."

He led her through another maze of short corridors, out of a door to where an old fire escape clung to the side of the building like black ivy.

She waited while he went through his ritual of lighting up.

"You served a couple last night a man who was with the woman on the left of this picture." She presented him with the picture of Michelle Armstrong and Janet Kerry.

He took it from her and stared down at the faces. "Aye, I remember her. She was with a guy in his late twenties or early thirties. Dark hair."

"Yes, we know who the man was. I was wondering if there was anything about them that caused you concern or seemed a bit off."

He handed back the photograph. "No, far from it. They seemed to be getting on really well. I got the impression at the start that they were on a first date." He paused to blow some smoke into the air. "They were a bit nervous at first but he gave her a white rose, which was pretty good. Most guys would have gone over the top with a dozen red but the white rose seemed classy. She looked pleased with it. As the meal wore on you could see they were talking more naturally and laughing together. What happened to them?"

The detail about the white rose was obviously significant. She replied to his question with a flat statement. "The woman was murdered."

"That's shite, she was nice." He dragged on the cigarette once more.

"Is there anything else you can tell me?"

"I'm afraid not. They were a pretty unremarkable couple, like loads we get here on a Friday night."

"Thanks for your time, Mr Gaughan. If you think of anything else don't hesitate to give me a ring." "She handed him her business card.

"Do you want me to show you the way out?"

"No, you finish your cigarette. I'm sure I'll find my way."

After a couple of wrong turns, Alex finally made her way back to the reception desk. As she was walking passed the receptionist called out, "Detective?"

"Yes," Alex said surprised to be summoned.

"Did you get what you were looking for?"

"I'm afraid not. I was looking for the contact details of one of the club's members, Nick Jackson. Your boss wasn't too keen to help."

The woman leaned forward and whispered, "She's a cow, isn't she?" For the benefit of a member of staff who was walking passed, in a louder voice she said, "I'll get you a membership form."

Intrigued, Alex watched as the woman went to a room at the side of the reception desk. She was gone for about five minutes. She returned bearing a membership form and below it a sheet of paper. When Alex looked at the paper she was pleased to see an address for Nick Jackson.

Reading from the woman's identity card, Alex said, "Thank you, Cathy. You're a very public-spirited citizen."

"You're welcome, but it didn't come from me."

"What didn't? Thanks for the membership form." Alex winked and left feeling that the investigation could now begin in earnest, and with any luck finish quickly.

*

Before they could do anything else they had to speak to Nick Jackson. On her arrival back at London Road, Alex detailed a couple of detectives to go pick up the suspect. DC Hendry had met a stubborn wall of silence with his request to the dating agency and was relieved when Alex told him that he didn't need to prepare the warrant request as she had obtained the information they needed.

Russell called her to his desk. "Watch this. This is from the CCTV on Royal Exchange Square." He clicked a play button on the screen of his computer. Alex guessed that someone else must have set it up for him, as he was notoriously bad with anything more complicated than a phone.

The digital clock on the screen showed 22:09 and the previous day's date.

"Here they come," Russell said, pointing to the couple as they walked along under the twinkling lights. Alex watched as Armstrong and Jackson paused for their discussion next to the statue.

"They stand there for about ten minutes," Russell commented, as he clicked on the fast forward button. Revellers, workers, boisterous students and a street sweeper rushed by at eight times normal speed until Russell click play again and everything returned to a more sedate pace.

The kiss that Michelle shared with Jackson was short and chaste but there was no doubting the warmth in it. Things had gone well, she was carrying the white rose and looked happy as she turned away from the camera. Jackson also turned away and walked in a different direction.

"He gave her the rose but there's not much to go on from that," Alex said disappointed.

"Watch," Russell insisted.

She focused on the screen once more and a short time later, sure enough Jackson reappeared into the shot and it was clear that he was now following the victim.

"It looks like Mr Jackson wasn't happy with just a wee peck on the cheek," Russell surmised.

"It doesn't mean he killed her."

"No, it doesn't but it is bloody suspicious." Russell looked eager to wrap the case up and some of his natural caution seemed to have gone. In the time that they had worked together, Russell had never been one to jump to quick conclusions but Alex had begun to believe that man was gone; he was but a memory.

"We'll see what he's got to say for himself," she said.

*

Despite the interview room being cool, Jackson was already sweating by the time the two detectives sat opposite him. He looked shell-shocked at the sudden upheaval of his life and Alex almost felt sorry for him, but the professional in her knew she had to put that aside as he could be a killer.

"Mr Jackson, I'm Detective Superintendent Russell and this is my colleague, Detective Inspector Menzies."

"Why am I here?" Jackson said, his voice quivering like a plucked guitar string.

Russell ignored the question, pressed the button on the tape recorder and announced who were present, then the date and the time. As Jackson wasn't under caution it wasn't strictly necessary, but Alex had seen Russell use the technique more than once before to unsettle a potential suspect, particularly one who had few, if any, dealings with the police before. As Jackson's record was clean, without even an outstanding parking ticket to his name, he was a prime candidate for the deception.

"Why are you doing that? I haven't done anything wrong," Jackson said, his body now trembling in sync with his voice.

"Standard procedure, Mr Jackson," Russell replied with cool detachment.

Jackson looked rapidly at each of them in turn. "I don't understand, why am I here?"

"Michelle Armstrong. I believe you took her for dinner last night." Russell's tone remained quiet and relatively gentle.

Jackson looked even more mystified as he said, "Michelle? What about her? Has something happened to her? Has she done something?" The questions rattled from him without a pause.

"Ms Armstrong was found dead this morning."

It was like Russell had physically assaulted him, so strong was his reaction. "What? No, no, no, that can't be right. You must be mistaken."

"No mistake, Mr Jackson, we have a confirmed identification. Would you like to tell me what happened last night? It'll be easier for you in the long run if you get it off your chest as soon as possible."

"Get it off my chest? Get what off my chest? We had a nice dinner, we talked, we said goodbye in the city centre about ten and then I went home."

"Not a good start, Jackson," Russell shouted, startling the shivering, fearful man. "That's a lie."

"No, it's not. That's what happened."

Russell was suddenly filled with growling menace as he leaned towards the suspect. "You're not very bright, are you son? We have CCTV pictures that prove otherwise. Now would you like to reconsider your statement?"

Jackson looked baffled before realising what it was that the detective was getting at. "I followed her to the underground station."

Russell leaned further forward, making him appear even more threatening. "Now look at it from my perspective. A man stalks a young woman after a date, and the following morning she turns up dead. Wouldn't you be suspicious?"

"It's not like that. I had offered to walk her to the station. I didn't think it was a good idea for her to walk alone through the city centre at that time of night. She said she would be fine and initially I let her go, but as I was walking away, I thought I would just keep an eye on her. So I followed her just to make sure she was safe."

"What a gent!" Russell said sarcastically. "Here's what I think happened. You pay for the fancy meal at your posh club and think to yourself that would be enough to guarantee you some payment in return. Then she gives you a wee peck on the cheek like you'd taken her to some dodgy fast-food restaurant for a cheap burger. That must have dented your ego, made you really angry. As you walked away you thought, no I'm getting what I paid for and you followed her, the rage pumping through your veins. When she still wouldn't give you what you wanted, you killed her, then panicked and came up with a plan to dump her body."

Jackson was more alarmed than angry as he shouted, "No, no, no. That's not what happened. I really liked her; I thought there was a genuine connection. It was a 'love at first sight' kind of thing. I was happy for things to go slowly because I thought I was going to see her again."

Russell sneered with a mocking laugh. "A good-looking, lad like you, you can't be used to getting your charms turned down, and it must have been devastating to that image you have of yourself. How dare she reject you."

Any small suggestion of composure Jackson might have had was now gone. "No! You don't know what you're talking about. Michelle was the first woman I had met through that bloody site who was more interested in who I am than what I earn. I liked her and I think she liked me. I did not kill her!"

"We have physical evidence that links you with where her body was found."

"What? You can't have."

"We have physical evidence from the crime scene that has your DNA on it." Alex realised that he was talking about the rose. He was stretching the truth, even if the forensics team did find Jackson's DNA on the flower, Roddy Gaughan would testify that Jackson had given Michelle the flower in perfectly innocent circumstances. Russell was playing the game, hoping Jackson would break due to the pressure that the detective was applying.

Jackson's face was now ashen. "You're lying. I had nothing to do with her death.

"You've no idea how often I've heard little shits like you tell me lies from the other side of a table just like this. You're a long way from being the best liar I've ever heard. Now for your sake and the sake of that lassie's family, tell me what really happened." It was another of Russell's interviewing techniques that Alex had heard many times before. His volume had increased to a shout and he slammed his hand on to the surface of the table bringing the sentence to an end with a very physical full stop.

"I want a lawyer," Jackson managed to whisper before his tremors overcame him completely.

"Interview terminated." Russell hammered the stop button and walked out the room without a word.

Alex was about to follow him when Jackson reached out and grabbed her arm with tightly clenched fingers. "Please detective, you've got to believe me, I didn't kill her."

"Remove your hand please, Mr Jackson," Alex said softly.

He withdrew his hand sharply. "I'm sorry. Please you've got to believe me." He began to cry, believing that his whole life was crumbling around him with astonishing speed.

She didn't reply, she simply left the room feeling more than a little sorry for the poor guy.

When she caught up with him, Russell's angry countenance told her all she needed to know. He didn't think that Jackson was their man and that meant the case was going to drag on. Once upon a time that wouldn't have bothered him, but now it was an inconvenience that meant more work than he could bring himself to care about.

"It's not him," she said simply as she sat down next to him.

"I know it's not him. Shit. He's scared of his own fuckin' shadow." He paused for a moment. "Move him out of that bloody interview room and once he's calmed down get somebody to take his statement. He might have seen something relevant."

Alex did as she was told, the detective she had chosen to interview Jackson as a possible witness was ordered to apologise to Jackson on their behalf when it was over. When she returned to his desk, there was no sign that her boss's mood had improved.

"What have we got?" he growled.

"Not a lot at the moment."

"What about the post mortem, any news when McNeill's going to get it done? At very least we need to know how she died. Maybe all we are dealing with is some nutcase failing to report a death by natural causes and deciding they would like a nice old funeral." His words dripped with resentment.

"I think that's unlikely, sir."

"Aw for fuck's sake, Alex, I know," he bellowed.

Months of pent up frustration and having bitten her tongue for so long suddenly burst from her in a torrent of rage. She shouted back, "There's no need to swear. I know life's been shitty for you, but I'm one of the few people who gives a damn what happens to you. I don't deserve your contempt and anger. I didn't kill Karen. I can't work with you if you're going to be shitty to me and everyone else around you. That's not what I signed up for."

The jibe about Karen only succeeded in stoking Russell's already boiling fury. "Well maybe you need to find somewhere else to work. Believe me it can be arranged."

"When this case is over, that'll suit me fine." She stormed away from him, sweeping up her bag and coat before charging out of the office and into her car. In the seclusion of the driver's seat, she screamed loudly and battered the steering wheel attracting a curious stare from a passing female PC. Before she drove away she called Noel and asked him if he wanted to come over to her place.

"Everything OK?" he asked concerned by her rage that seethed down the line.

"I'll explain it later. Bring in a pizza and a large bottle of red, please."

"Will do, see you soon."

Meanwhile, in the office, the other detectives were trying hard not to catch Russell's eye, everyone was suddenly intent on their particular task, finding fascination in witness statements and delight in the details of a spreadsheet.

For his part, Russell was already regretting his outburst. *What the hell is wrong with me?* was all he could think.

His phone rang and he was going to ignore it until he realised it was the mortuary.

'Russell."

"Superintendent Russell, it's Eilidh McNeill."

"Yes Doctor," he muttered.

"The PM will be tomorrow at ten thirty."

"That's fine. I'll get someone along."

When the call was over, he sent a text with the details to Alex, asking her to attend. He didn't send an apology; he would have to do that face-to-face when he saw her in the morning. As for his angry alternate ego, he would have to be dealt with soon for the sake of everyone. The problem was he had no idea where to start.

CHAPTER 5

When his day of work had come to its end, Russell went in to his local supermarket and bought a bottle of Highland Park Malt Whisky. With no interest in cooking, his dinner was a cheese and ham sandwich accompanied by a mug of tea.

Two hours later he was sitting in what had become a customary position staring at the alcohol, trying to decide whether tonight it was his friend or his enemy.

His head was filled with thoughts of his argument with his DI. He knew that Alex was as good a detective as he had ever worked with, and he had enjoyed their time together; they made a good team. After the way he had treated her he couldn't blame her if she wanted to escape from the person he had become.

He also wished that he could leave behind that personality. Sometimes he felt there was someone else in control of his emotions and his mouth; he would say things and it would sound like a stranger talking. Tonight had been one more episode where the alien voice had taken over and made him sound like a man who wished to push people away. He knew that if it continued in the same manner it was not sustainable, he would inevitably say or do something to the wrong person and it would end his career in ignominy.

"I think it's time to write that resignation letter, Tommy boy," he said into the empty room.

The very action of voicing his thoughts, even if it was just to himself, felt like a release, a breaking of the bonds he had created for himself. He would see this case out, resign and recommend that Alex replace him. It was the least he could do for her. His only concern was that he would be unable to rebuild their relationship in the time he had left; tonight was the final act in a disagreement that had been simmering for some months.

He lifted the glass and the whisky, put them back into the kitchen cupboard, feeling that a weight had been lifted. He went back into the living room, flicked through his CD collection until he found a recording of Mozart's Requiem Mass. He put the CD in the tray, pressed play and switched off all the lights. He sat in the dark and let the melancholy music wash over him, playing it on repeat until late into the night.

*

Sunday morning dawned warm and bright, with brilliant sunshine and the promise of a glorious day ahead. Alex never liked visiting the mortuary but it somehow always felt worse on a day like this. A day when people were full of life; taking their kids to the park or the beach; walking in the country; cycling beside the river; or just inviting friends and family for an impromptu barbecue. Michelle Armstrong would never experience those things again; today she would be cut open to allow Dr McNeill to tell the story of her murder. Today the story of her life was irrelevant; it was only her death that mattered.

During the previous evening Noel had helped to dispel the anger she was feeling towards Russell; he had listened patiently and made suggestions that allowed Alex time to reflect and consider what should happen next.

However, she wasn't ready to face the detective superintendent just yet and had arranged to meet Ann-Marie Craigan at Helen Street station - their base when they weren't working a case somewhere across the country.

She drove the short trip from the station to the mortuary that was situated in the grounds of the new South Glasgow Hospital. The detective sergeant told her about the sad duty of telling Michelle's mother and father of the death of their daughter. Mrs Armstrong had fainted when they went to identify Michelle's body; Ann-Marie said she had liked the couple and that the whole experience had been as wretched as anything she had done in her career.

Doctor McNeill and her colleague Dr Rajesh Gupta conducted the post mortem. It took nearly two hours and by the end of it, the pathologist concluded that Michelle Armstong had died of asphyxiation, probably as a result of poisoning. The dilation of her pupils was noted as a sign of something toxic in her system. Dilation is one of the symptoms of any number of poisons that affect the nervous system, and therefore did not provide a definitive answer as to what had killed the woman. Almost every ingested poison results in vomiting, with some causing the victim to foam at the mouth. Due to the lack of any sign of vomit on the body or the dress, Dr McNeill reckoned that the body had been both washed and redressed. It would take further tests before the deadly substance could be identified. The doctor told the detectives that the key to finding what killed the young woman now lay in the forensic labs. Histology and toxicology would hopefully provide the vital key to the woman's death that the PM had not identified. There was a large forensic lab in the floors above the mortuary, but as it was Sunday the chances of getting results that day were remote. Alex thanked both pathologists and then dropped Ann-Marie back at Helen Street where she had left her own car.

She was not looking forward to telling Russell that they still didn't know how Michelle Armstrong had died other than the vague cause of poisoning. If he was in the same mood as he had been the last time she had spoken to him, it was going to be hellish.

Some of her concern disappeared as she walked into the incident room. Russell looked to be a little less stressed but the news Alex was bringing might make him think about shooting the messenger.

"Good afternoon, Alex. How did it go?"

"Good afternoon, sir. Not brilliantly, I'm afraid."

The story of the post mortem didn't last long but Russell was more resigned than angry.

"We'll just need to wait for the test results. Alex, can I have a word?"

He stood up and walked into the corridor. Alex followed and watched while he tried a few office doors before he found one that was open and empty. He invited his DI to join him, and once inside the room moved to the window and rested his back against it.

"I'm sorry about last night, I was out of order," he said with his arms folded across his chest.

"I'm sorry too," she replied.

"No, there's no need, you've nothing to apologise for. I honestly don't know who I am anymore. I spent a lot of time thinking last night, considering my future and I came to the conclusion that it's time for me to go. I've decided to resign when this case is closed."

Although she had thought it possible, his words still came as a bit of a shock. "No, you can't."

"I need to, Alex. I can't go on like this. Every body we have to look at will be a reminder of my failure, a failure that cost the life of the only woman that I ever loved. She haunts me, Alex. She disturbs my sleep, there are reminders of her everywhere when I'm awake and she's at the forefront of my thoughts at every crime scene. I can't do the job properly if my mind is not on the victim but is instead processing all that I did wrong. I can't be a good detective if I live in constant fear of another failure."

"Sir, you're not thinking straight. You need to address what's wrong, not run away from it. I know the psychologist you went to wasn't the best, but there are better people out there who can help you."

"I'll be honest with you, I don't know if I even have the energy to try. I looked at the girl in the cemetery yesterday and all I could see was Karen. I used to be able to get a sense of the criminal from his crime, but it's like that ability has gone, surrendered to grief, or maybe it's just been suppressed by my own guilt and the influence of another killer. Whatever the reason, I can't function as a detective any more."

Alex became passionate in her attempt to change his mind. "All the more reason that you need to confront it. You can't let the guilt you feel become you. You need to know that you didn't kill Karen, that bastard Dent did. How many of the real bad guys have you put away? How many victims' families have you helped by getting them some form of justice? That's what you should be focusing on."

"Thanks for your concern, but my mind's made up. For now keep this between us, I'll tell the ACC when this is over."

"I think you're wrong, we need you," she pleaded sadly, but it she could see by the determined set of his face that it was in vain.

'We better get on,' he said.

They returned to the incident room where Russell turned his attention to the whiteboard. Michelle Armstrong's picture had been joined by a number of Noel's shots from the crime scene. He had taken pictures of the corpse in its funereal pose from a number of angles. There was something Gothically macabre about the whole scene, like Miss Havisham had finally escaped her long wait for her groom. Dickens tragic heroine lifted from the pages and laid to rest on a weather-beaten gravestone.

The photographer had also taken some pictures after the body had been removed. The text on the stone was now visible through its coat of bottle green moss.

Alex had joined Russell to survey the board. "Look at this," she said pointing to a picture of the stone that had three names on it but one in particular had caught her attention.

She read aloud what had been inscribed. "Sarah Maitland, Born 12th February 1868, Died 14th August 1893."

"So?" Russell asked looking puzzled.

"I was wondering why the killer had placed Michelle's body on this particular grave. He could have left it on the first grave next to the gate. Why did he drive that far into the cemetery and increase the chances of being caught? That girl, Sarah Maitland, she was about the same age as Michelle. I'm just wondering if there is something else that they have in common."

"Like what?" Ann-Marie Craigan had joined them, intrigued by what Alex was saying.

"What about the way they died?"

"You think that the killer has copied a Victorian crime?" Russell asked.

"I'm not sure, but it might be worth a look. There had to be some reason he picked that particular grave," Alex argued.

"As we've not got much else to go on it's worth having a look. See what you can find," Russell suggested. "I need to check how the evidence gathering has been going."

"You up for it, Ann-Marie?" Alex asked.

"You bet I am."

The two women settled down at the nearest computer and began their search for details of Sarah Maitland. The search engine returned a number of entries for a variety of Sarah Maitlands across the globe in the form of LinkedIn and other social media profiles. On the fourth page of results they finally found what they were looking for on a site dedicated to unsolved murders.

THE POISONED BRIDE

Sarah Maitland, daughter of Glaswegian tea retailer, David Maitland, was killed by poison on the eve of her wedding to Albert Reynolds in August of 1893. The police investigation focused on her bridesmaid, Elise Watkins, who had been betrothed to Reynolds before he fell in love with her best friend. Although she was tried for murder, the jury returned a verdict of 'not proven' - a verdict unique to Scotland - due to a lack of evidence and she went free. Watkins died in 1935, Before she died she confessed to her lawyer that she had indeed killed her friend in a fit of jealousy.

Ann-Marie Craigan printed the web page and Alex took it to Russell. He read it and when he was finished removed his glasses and pinched the bridge of his nose.

"What does this tell us?"

"We need more detail, but surely it can't be a coincidence. The age, the wedding dress, as well as the fact that the doc believes Michelle was poisoned," Alex enthused, even though she wasn't sure exactly what the connection was or why someone would wish to copy such an old crime.

Russell's fatigued expression was a mirror for the intellectual fugue he was feeling. Thinking was difficult as his mind was exhausted. "I doubt that the criminal record still exists but we might get something from the newspapers of the day. It's probably worth a visit to the Mitchell Library."

"It's Sunday, it'll be closed." Alex replied.

"Shit. OK that's a task for tomorrow. Has anyone interviewed the family yet?"

"No, sir. I didn't think that yesterday was the right time," DS Craigan replied.

"You're right Ann-Marie, but we need to fill in the victim's background if we're going to find possible reasons for her death. Alex, go with Ann-Marie to see what they've got to say."

"Will do."

The two women left and Russell tried to find some energy from somewhere. He would need to write a report for the ACC but he was lacking both motivation and drive. Instead of compiling the report, he went for a walk to try to clear his head.

CHAPTER 6

They were on yet another journey to see yet another family, yet another collection of shattered lives that would never be made whole again. Over the years Alex had evolved her own cloak of emotional protection, but in almost every case where crime destroyed the lives of good people, there would be a little flaw in that cloak that allowed their pain to affect her. She put on the mental shield as they made their way to the interview.

When the two detectives arrived at the family home in Knightswood there were cars parked all along the street radiating from the front of the Armstrong house.

A short, silver-haired woman opened the door, dressed respectfully in black.

Alex introduced herself and her colleague.

"We were wondering if there's any chance that we could speak to Mr and Mrs Armstrong?"

"Come away in pet. Ah'm Netta, Elsie's sister."

"Thank you."

The older lady led the detectives into a living room full of people. The house was already packed with family and friends who had rallied around to offer what little they could, whether it was emotional strength or physical help. Some of them looked morose, some were trying to maintain some level of normality, while others were in the kitchen, spreading sandwiches and making tea.

When the detectives walked in, the room fell into silence.

Netta announced them, "Elsie, hen. These lassies ur fae the polis. They want tae huv a word wi' ye aboot Michelle."

Mrs Armstrong looked up, and Alex's cloak failed to protect her from the wave of grief that radiated from the woman. No pain can match the loss of a child, and Mrs Armstrong looked like every bone, muscle and nerve was racked with an ache so all encompassing and so deep that she would live with it for the rest of her life.

"Does this really have to be done now?" asked a young man wearing the black garb of a priest. He was backed up by murmurs of agreement from some of those present.

Alex replied with polite strength. "I'm sorry Father, but the sooner we can get more information about Michelle, the more likely we are to catch her killer."

"It's awright, Father Muldoon, we'll answer the questions," a broad-shouldered, angular man said as he stood up. In turn he offered the detectives his hand and introduced himself to Alex. "Kenny Armstrong."

"We're sorry for your loss Mr Armstrong, Mrs Armstrong. Is there somewhere where we can speak privately?"

"We'll go ben the room." He bent to help his wife to her feet and he held her arm as she shuffled as if in a daze through to the hall and into a bedroom.

Mrs Armstrong was already seated on the bed by the time Craigan and Menzies entered. There was a single chair close to the window and Mr Armstrong invited Alex to take a seat. Michelle's mother, dressed all in black, was a small, plump woman with dazzling white hair. Her blue eyes were tinged with red, her cheeks slack in grief. She wore a heavy musky perfume, a scent that dominated the room.

"I'll go speak to the F.L.O.," Ann-Marie Craigan said. She had decided to make the interview a little less intimidating for the Armstrongs, so a visit to the Family Liaison Officer. was as good an excuse as any.

"Thanks, DS Craigan," Alex said, appreciating her colleague's understanding.

Kenny Armstrong had taken his place beside his wife and held her hand as he looked intently at Alex. He looked to be a little older than his wife. His gaunt features were grey and black rings surrounded his eyes. He was dressed formally in a white shirt and black tie with dark blue suit trousers. His shoes were highly polished, his pride in his appearance was still intact despite the evident agonies he was feeling at his daughter's death.

"Whit cin we dae fur ye, hen?" he asked.

"I know this is difficult for you and that this is the worst possible time for me to be here, but it is essential that we get some idea of who might have wanted to harm your daughter. The quicker we can move on an investigation like this, the more likely we are to catch the culprit."

He nodded. "Aye, it's awright, we understaun'."

"Did Michelle ever tell you about anyone that she felt uncomfortable with or that she had had an argument with? Someone who may have wanted to harm her."

Mrs Armstrong shook her head and found her voice. "Naw, Ah don't think so."

Her husband also indicated his lack of knowledge. "Oor Michelle wis an easy goin' lassie, she wid go oot o' her way tae avoid arguments."

Alex tried to prompt a memory by saying, "This might not have been recent. This might be someone who was holding a long-term grudge."

Again both parents replied in the negative.

"Tell me a little about Michelle. Did she have many friends?"

"Aye, quite a few. She liked folk and folk liked her," Mr Armstrong said, his pride in his daughter was clear to see.

His wife said, "She wis always quite outgoin'. Up 'til the accident onyway."

"Accident?"

Mr Armstrong took up the story. "Aye, couple o' year ago a boy stepped oot in front o' her oan Great Western Road. It wis late at night and he wis steamin'. There wis nothin' oor Michelle could dae aboot it. She hit him and he wis killed."

"What happened?"

"The polis were involved but there wis aboot twinty folk who witnessed it. They aw said that the lad wis staggerin', tripped and then stumbled oot between two parked moators."

"So Michelle never faced any charges?"

"Naw, it wisnae her fault. She wis under the speed limit, she hudnae been drinkin' or nothin'. It wis jist the way his heid clattered the grun that killed him. Polis said it was a freak accident, 'cause maist folk that get hit at that speed normally end up wi' jist broken bones. It's rare fur it tae be fatal, so they telt us."

"But the accident had an effect on Michelle?"

Mrs Armstrong said, "She never drove efter that, even though it wisnae her fau't. She wis awfy withdrawn fur a while. She felt guilty aboot whit hud happened, even though she couldnae huv prevented it. Getting that wee café gaun with Janet wis the best thing that happened tae her. It brought her oot her shell again, allowed her tae go oot mair." She realised what she had said, and her tears began to fall once again.

The next question was awkward but needed to be asked. "Did Michelle ever have any problems with the victim's family?"

Mr Armstrong replied forcefully, "Naw, not at all. She wrote them a letter apologising fur whit happened, but ye know whit happened?"

Mr Armstrong seemed to expect a reply, so Alex shook her head.

"They wrote back and apologised tae her. Said their son wis a waster and that if it hudnae been the accident, it wid huv been somethin' else, a fight or drugs. That's whit they said, cin ye believe it?"

Alex felt that his incredulity was spot on. Could someone really lose a son in an accident and then blame him? She thought it unlikely but maybe his parents had reached the end of their tether. Even if his parents had given up on him, Alex was sure that there would be plenty of people he would have known that would happily blame Michelle. A possible motive had emerged.

"Do you know the man's name?"

"Eh… whit wis it again? Allen. Kyle Allen."

Alex took a note of the name.

"Do you have the address of his family? I'd like to talk to them."

"It'll be on Michelle's computer, hen. Janet'll huv it at their flat."

"That's fine, we picked up the computer yesterday. Is there anything you'd like to ask me?"

Mrs Armstrong looked to her husband and gripped his hand tighter.

"We wanted tae know, did they, ye know, interfere wi' her?" he asked.

"No, there was no assault of that kind." Alex was relieved that she could give that reply honestly. Dr McNeill had said explicitly that Michelle had not suffered in that way.

"Wis she in much pain afore she passed?" Mrs Armstrong asked, her voice just above a whisper.

The lie was easy to tell. "There's no evidence that she suffered, no." Protecting the victim's family from the worst details of a murder was one skill that all detectives had to use regularly.

"Ah suppose that's somethin' tae be thankful tae God fur." She made the sign of the cross with her right hand.

Alex never ceased to be amazed at the faith people could have at the point where their God had let them down so devastatingly, but, she thought if it would help the Armstrongs through this most trying time, that was all that really mattered.

"Anything else?"

"When will we be allowed tae bury her?"

"There are still a few tests to be done to establish how she died but it shouldn't be too long."

"Thanks, hen."

"The family liaison officer will keep you informed and if there's anything we can do to help just ask him and we'll see what we can do."

"Thanks hen."

Alex stood to leave but before she could get out of the room, Mrs Armstrong reached for her hand.

"Please find who did this tae ma wee lassie. Please promise me ye'll dae aw ye cin."

"I promise, Mrs Armstrong. We'll do everything we can."

Alex collected the detective sergeant from the kitchen, said goodbye to Netta and the family liaison officer before heading back to London Road.

*

"I don't believe a word of it," Russell said when Alex told him about the letter. "How does anybody suffering that kind of grief just turn around and forgive a killer, even if it was an accident?"

She immediately thought that his attitude resulted directly from his own recent experience. He would be unable to see it from anyone else's perspective, although she did understand his scepticism.

"I think we've got to take a closer look at it. It might not be his direct family who are involved. Maybe a mate or a more distant relative."

"The details will be on the database. Here, you operate this thing or we'll be here all day."

He left his desk and Alex replaced him on the chair. She began the process of logging in to the database and setting up the search details.

She typed in Kyle Allen; the code for a road traffic accident and a six-month time span for about two years ago. The little sand-timer cursor turned slowly on the screen while the parameters were passed to and from the server.

After about a minute of waiting, and increasing impatience from Russell, the results appeared.

'Here we go," Alex observed.

The fields she had used were specific enough to return a single result.

The two of them read the report, Russell nodding to Alex to move the page down when he was ready.

Kyle Allen had been drinking since two o'clock in the afternoon when he left the pub on Great Western Road at half-past ten on the night of the accident. Witnesses reported that he had been very unsteady on his feet and was slurring his words. He staggered across the pavement, missed his footing on the kerb and as he tried to regain his balance he stumbled into the road between two parked cars. Michelle Armstrong had almost no time to react and she could do nothing other than hit him. The impact threw his head backwards on to the tarmac and the resulting collision between the road and his skull had caused a massive brain haemorrhage. The attached pathologist's report - written by Doctor Gupta - indicated that it was his belief that death would have been instantaneous. The victim's blood alcohol count was recorded at some eight times the legal limit for driving as it was defined at the time when the incident occurred.

The investigating officer's summary attributed no blame to Michelle Armstrong and Alex commented, "Definitely a tragic accident."

"Aye. Let's have a look at Mr Allen's record, if he's got one."

Alex's fingers flew across the keyboard at a speed Russell could only dream of. It wasn't too long before they had Kyle Allen's police record, and it was filled with plenty of information.

Russell noted, "He was quite a lad was Mr Allen."

He was only nineteen when he died, but his charge sheet had entries stretching back six years including vandalism, car theft, drug offences and common assault.

"A waster," was Russell's verdict.

"It must have been tough on his folks. Maybe they did give up on him."

"I'm pretty sure with that record, there were plenty of scumbag pals that didn't think Michelle Armstrong was so innocent. We should check if any of his known associates have been serving time for the past couple of years and are back on the streets."

"Do you think they're likely to come up with something so elaborate?"

"Probably not, but they're not all as thick as shit, and maybe one of them thought that they would throw us off the scent. I know, it's unlikely, but as I know to my cost, revenge is a very strong motive."

He moved away from the desk and called the detectives who were in the room to the incident board. All that had been discovered during the day was added to the collection and the information briefed to the team. New tasks were allocated for the following day. Alex would pay a visit to Kyle Allen's parents checking out whether any of Kyle Allen's pals had a criminal record and if so to interview them. DS Craigan would lead a team that would be investigating any known associates of Allen. DC Hendry was tasked with finding the source of the wedding dress. If the killer had bought it recently from either a charity shop or a theatrical costumier, there was a chance a paper trail would lead back to his door. To Alex's surprise, Russell informed them that he would be paying a visit to the Mitchell Library. It wasn't a true part of the investigation, more a background check that may offer some context but at least he was going to be out of the office.

Russell ended the meeting by telling the officers to go home, rest and be ready to start again fresh in the morning.

*

An hour after the rest of the team had gone home, Russell was still plodding through a report for the ACC on his computer. The door swung open and he looked up to see Catriona Carmichael framed in the doorway.

"Still hard at it, Tom?" she asked.

"Just finishing another performance report for the bean counter."

"Would you like to go for something to eat?"

He wasn't sure he was ready for company. "I should really finish this."

"Come on, it'll be there in the morning. His lordship is too wrapped up in preparing for his next press appearance to bother anyway. My treat. There's a great wee Italian I know."

As Catriona was an old friend whom he didn't want to offend and as he didn't feel like cooking, he decided that there would be no harm in it. "Fair enough."

She offered to drive. Fifteen minutes later they were in a tiny Italian restaurant in the Merchant City. She was obviously a regular customer as the waiter greeted her by name and chatted to her with comfortable familiarity. When they were seated, they were supplied with a complimentary bowl of olives served with focaccia bread, which they nibbled on as they consulted the menu.

On Catriona's recommendation, he ordered seafood risotto. A bottle of Pinot Grigio arrived and when the wine was poured, Catriona raised her glass and said, "To better times."

During the meal they chatted of their days in uniform and in particular their time pounding the beat in Springburn. She reminded him of the night that they were stopped by a very angry old man who said that every time he turned on the hot water tap on his bath, he could hear 'Agadoo'. He was convinced that someone had wired the tap to drive him mad. The two constables had told him it was not a matter for the police and referred him to his landlord.

The anecdotes took Russell back to simpler times free of weighty responsibility and their conviviality helped him to relax. For the first time in what felt like ages, he laughed. A genuine laugh, free of pretence or the strain of putting on a face for the sake of others.

While they were enjoying their dessert, Catriona said, "Would you like to come back to my flat for a coffee?"

"Flat?"

"Yes. Bill and his new flame are in the house. As part of the divorce, he'll buy my half. I'm renting a place about five minutes from here."

"Oh, right." Russell wasn't sure what to say. This all felt so strange compared with his almost hermit-like existence since his divorce. When he considered the reality of the loneliness of his cold, empty flat and the thought of another staring contest with the whisky, the decision was made. "That would be nice, thank you."

They walked towards her home in a light shower of rain that relieved some of the oppressive humidity that had built up in the city over the course of the day. The pessimistic Glaswegian in Russell made him think that the city would pay for this spell of warm, late summer weather. Freezing cold and pouring rain was probably not too far away.

Catriona's flat was on the first floor above a designer clothes shop. Her home was bright and felt spacious although it was much the same size as Russell's own - the decor made it look cheerful and more welcoming.

"Can you stick the coffee on, while I get out of this uniform?" Catriona asked.

"Sure."

"The percolator is next to the hob and the coffee's in the second cupboard on the right."

He walked into the simple little kitchen - it didn't look like it was used for cooking very often - and made the coffee as instructed. The percolator started to bubble and soon the smell of a rich, nutty roast filled the flat.

As it brewed, Catriona walked back in wearing a bright pink T-shirt and a pair of black jeans. Her hair was down and loose, free of the formal style she wore while working. Russell was stunned by how good she looked. Like all homogeneous clothing, a police uniform had a habit of hiding the person underneath, but now that she had cast it aside, Russell could see who she really was, and he was impressed.

Coffee poured, they sat beside each other on a sofa in the living room.

The weight of his decision to resign was pressing on him and he had a sudden urge to divulge his plan to this woman who had been in and out of his working life for his whole career. He felt she was someone who would understand and that he could trust.

When he finished telling her of his resolve to resign and the reasoning behind it, she said firmly, "No, that's a very bad idea."

"Why?"

"It's not you that made that decision, it's the emotional monster that's had a grip of you for the past year. The one that consumes you every night, and that you allow to win without a fight." She leaned closer to him, "You're still a good man Tom Russell, and a bloody good copper." She kissed him, long and hard. After his initial surprise, he began to kiss her back.

She put her coffee on the small table and stood up suddenly. He thought he had misunderstood, but she lifted his coffee from his hand, placed it beside her own and urged him to stand up. She led him through to the bedroom where she kissed him once again with the intense passion of some-one who had been bereft of a physical relationship for some time. He responded in kind and they began to undress each other.

They made love with gentle caresses and ardent kisses, each movement considered and thoughtful. Catriona could feel every tense knot in his muscles pressing against her soft flesh. She subtly massaged his stress-riven body and felt him relax further.

It had been a few years since Russell had been with a woman. There never had been anyone after Karen; he thought that part of his life was over. Catriona's patience and understanding, the tenderness of her touch and warmth of her embrace made him feel something he hadn't been capable of for a very long time; a sense of peace.

When they had both climaxed, it was as if something in Russell's psyche broke free from the strictures he had placed on it. He started to weep; the tears became sobs, deep and heartfelt. He buried his head in her breasts and wept like a child for a full hour, while she gently cradled him in her arms and shared his grief. When the tears dried up, Catriona said, "Tell me about her."

Slowly, thoughtfully he said, "We met at a party, a Hogmanay party in fact. She was the most stunning woman in the room. We chatted and I asked her out. We were married within two years. She was a kind person but she was always jealous, irrationally so. She didn't realise that she was the only woman I wanted to be with, there was an insecurity about her that eventually began to drive a wedge between us. It was probably my fault. I didn't tell her how much she meant to me."

His melancholy returned and Catriona saw her opportunity. "What happened on the day she died?"

For the first time since that day, Russell talked openly about the Harlequin and Karen's death. His helplessness, his anger, the despair and his guilt all came tumbling out in a torrent of words. She allowed him to talk uninterrupted, letting him fill the silence when it occurred and gently coaxing him into revealing all that he had felt since that tragic day.

When he had finally told her everything, exhausted, he fell asleep in her arms.

CHAPTER 7

Despite having slept for only four hours, Russell awoke having rested in a way that he had thought he had lost forever. He noticed that Catriona was already up and in the kitchen; the smell of fresh coffee was once more drifting in to the bedroom.

He put on his underwear, shirt and trousers, and walked through to the living room.

"Good morning," she said.

"Good morning." Russell had no idea what to say beyond the simple response.

"Did you sleep well?"

"Yes I did, thanks."

"How are you feeling?"

"Embarrassed, guilty, fearful," he replied honestly.

Concerned, she asked, "Why?"

"Embarrassed that I cried for so long and unburdened myself to you, fearful that you might resent me for it, and guilty that I enjoyed what came before the tears."

She handed him a coffee and a croissant.

"You have nothing to be embarrassed about. You finally confronted that demon you've been carrying around with you for a long time. I didn't make love with you last night out of some sense of pity. I did it because you are a man I have known, liked and admired for some time. I don't jump into bed with just anyone you know." She finished her speech with a reassuring smile.

"I'm just confused. You're the first woman I've been to bed with apart from Karen. If anyone had said to me at this time yesterday that I would end up spending the night with you, I'd have said they were nuts. I don't know what happened to change that. It's all a bit of a confused haze."

"Tom, you have to understand that reaching out to ask for help or comfort from another human being is not a sign of weakness. What we did last night was two lonely human beings making a real connection, beyond just sex. When you told me that you were going to quit the force and the reason behind it, you let me see just how much pain you were in. I have my own stuff to deal with. Despite our divorce being pretty amicable, there's a big part of me that knows I let Bill down. I've carried that guilt and I've felt lonely since we separated. I needed to connect with another human being completely and when you walked into my office, I saw the face of a friend. I needed you and, I think, without realising it you needed me. That's why you told me your story, you were reaching out."

"That doesn't sound like me." He replied and managed a weak smile of his own.

"You have to realise that last night wasn't the end of the pain you feel, it was the first stage of a journey back to you. I hope you'll let me walk it with you. What do you think?"

"I don't know what to say. This is a lot to take in. Why would you want to?"

"Because, you silly man, you're a friend. I would like to have someone to share my life with in some way, and I would prefer that it is a good man. As I said last night, you are a good man Tom Russell and you deserve to be happy. Let's see if we can help make each other happy."

"You seem to have thought a lot about this."

"I didn't sleep much last night."

"I'm not sure you know what you would be letting yourself in for."

"I'm not suggesting any huge commitment beyond dinner, conversation and friendship. I ask just one thing from you."

"What's that?"

"That you speak to a professional that can help you deal with what you've been through."

"I don't know Catriona, it's difficult for me to speak to a stranger and I didn't have much luck with the last professional I spoke to."

"I'm willing to help you, Tom but I can't do it alone. Please tell me you'll think about it at least."

He nodded. "What happens now?"

"We finish our breakfast, you have a shower and then we go to work."

He laughed, "I meant about us."

"We take life as it comes and see where it leads us."

*

Alex's visit to Kyle Allen's family proved to be fruitless. His mother told the detective that she had known for sometime that her son's behaviour would lead to something terrible happening. She bore Michelle Armstrong no malice. She was actually saddened to hear of her death.

The detective returned to the office and almost immediately she could tell that something about Russell was different. The careworn, troubled look he had sported for much of the recent past seemed to be etched a little less deeply in his face. He was wearing the same shirt as the previous day. That was very uncharacteristic and it was an observation that piqued Alex's interest.

"Good morning, sir."

"Good morning, Alex. How was your trip?"

'It was a complete waste of time. It's just like the Armstrongs said. Mrs Allen didn't blame Michelle for Kyle's death. She did give me a list of his friends, so I'll have a look at them, see if there's a villain among them."

"I'm heading to the Mitchell to check up on this Sarah Maitland thing. Let me know if anything crops up."

"Sure."

She would have to get to the bottom of what had happened to him, the detective in her demanded it.

*

For over a hundred years the Mitchell has been the biggest and most important library in the city. Its distinctive and imposing green dome dominates the area overlooking the M8 motorway at Charing Cross.

Russell entered the building on Granville Street, which leads to the Mitchell Theatre and the broad expanse of the modern café that also hosted Internet access terminals.

He made his way to the reception on the first floor and told the young man what he needed. He directed him to the archives section, he was told that someone there would help him with the records he was looking for.

A red-haired man with an extravagant Edwardian-style beard greeted him at the reception desk of the reference section.

"My name is Detective Superintendent Tom Russell, I'm looking for some help."

"Tim Lauchlan," the librarian replied as he shook Russell's hand. "What do you need?"

After Russell had told him the information he was looking for, Lauchlan said, "That's quite a cold case." His face cracked into a broad smile.

"It's not a case as such," Russell said.

"It must be fascinating being a detective. I've always fancied being a bit of a Poirot, myself."

"It's not really as glamorous as television, more tedious and mundane," Russell replied politely.

"I'm sure you're being modest. If you follow me, I'll take you to the archives."

Russell did as requested while the man kept up a constant monologue as he searched for the relevant microfiche films. "Is this something to do with the girl that was found in the graveyard? I suppose it must be but you won't be able to talk about it. You can't comment on an on-going investigation;

they always say that on the telly. I wonder how she died, the papers haven't said, but I suppose you need to keep that a secret so it's only you and the killer that know. I wonder how someone can do that, take another person's life, I mean. You must ask yourselves that a lot."

The detective ignored the librarian's inanities and finally Lauchlan announced, "Ah, here we are."

He pulled a reel from a box and walked to the viewer. Once he had loaded the spool, he said, "If you need anything else, just let me know. Good luck catching the killer."

He walked away and Russell muttered, "I thought librarians preferred silence."

It wasn't easy to see the details of the text as it zoomed past as he turned the control of the spooling mechanism.

Finally, a bit of technology I know how to operate, he thought.

The images sped past for some time until he reached August of 1893, at which point he slowed the speed at which he turned the handle. Eventually he spotted what he had been looking for.

Russell reversed the turn until the article appeared. It was written in a strangely formal Victorian style.

MYSTERIOUS AFFAIR IN MOUNT VERNON
- BRIDE POISONED ON EVE OF WEDDING -
During last week Mount Vernon and its vicinity have been in a state of excitement in consequence of Miss Sarah Maitland, being the daughter of Mr. David Maitland, residing at Mansionhouse Road, having been poisoned by partaking of sherry. About two weeks

since, the boy of Mr. Muir, grocer, brought to the house a bottle of sherry. On the eve of Miss M's nuptials Mrs. Elizabeth Maitland organised a family dinner in celebration of her daughter's marriage. In attendance were Mr M. his wife, their elder daughter Miss Charlotte Maitland, Miss Sarah Maitland and her friend Miss Elise Watkins, who was to be the bridesmaid of Miss Maitland.

After the completion of the meal, Miss Watkins served the sherry to the ladies. The youngest daughter had no sooner swallowed a portion of the drink than she complained of a heat in the mouth and throat. She was shortly taken ill, and, to allay the violent heat she procured water and drank it. Miss C.M at the request of her father instantly proceeded to a surgeon, to require his attendance. Dr Douglas proceeded to her residence, where he found Miss S.M. in a dreadful state, and apparently in a serious condition. Although Miss M had only partaken of a single glass of sherry, she was attacked with sickness. About 8 o'clock, she vomited and was riven by great convulsions and spasms. She was in a dreadful condition of seizure, and could scarcely speak. She requested to be left alone. When Dr D. again called (about 9 o'clock) he found Miss Maitland lying on her bed quite dead.

On Monday morning of this week Mr Kenneth, surgeon, stated that on Friday he attended a post mortem examination of the deceased lady, and was of opinion that her death was occasioned by poison. He had examined a quantity of the decanted sherry that was sent to him for his examination on Thursday, but he could not detect any sort of poison. - Dr Douglas, surgeon, had analysed the glass from which Miss Sarah Maitland had consumed the sherry, and found it to contain traces of the strychnine.

Mr George McMurdo, a chymist - Two weeks last Saturday, a woman called at my shop, and asked for two ounces of mercury, and afterwards for an ounce of calomel. I refused to let her have it, and made her up 12 one-grain calomel pills. - Mr Johnson, of Tollcross, chymist - Last Monday week, a young lady called at my house and asked me for an ounce of arsenic and an ounce of salts. I refused to furnish her with the articles, I asked her if she knew the nature of arsenic, and she replied, "Oh, yes, perfectly," and smiled. I then labelled the packet "poison." - Miss Elise Watkins resembled the lady, but he would not swear positively to her. Mr Jenkins, chymist, stated, that about 11 days ago a young lady came into his shop and asked for an ounce of salts and an ounce of arsenic, the latter she said was to destroy beetles. He refused to let her have the arsenic, as it appeared singular to him that she should want to destroy such beetles at this time of year. John Whatlock, assistant to Mrs Maddocks, chymist and druggist - About ten or twelve days ago a young lady came into our shop, and asked for an ounce of salts. She then asked for an ounce of strychnine, for the purpose of killing mice. I refused to serve her.

Dr Douglas was of the opinion that the poison was mixed with the sherry during the pouring of the drink.

*Miss Elise Watkins is to face trial by jury and will face
a charge of Wilful murder.*

Russell noted that Ms Watkins having failed to purchase
arsenic, instead switched to strychnine.

She was determined; I'll give her that, he thought.

He wondered if there was a record of what happened at
her trial so he began to spool once more.

*THE GLASGOW BRIDE POISONING CASE
THE TRIAL OF MISS ELISE WATKINS
This trial, which has been for some time looked forward
to with intense interest - the prisoner being a young lady
lately moving in respectable circles in Glasgow, and the
fatal event being the supposed issue of a romantic at-
tachment - commenced before the High Court Of Jus-
ticiary at Edinburgh on the 21st. The court was filled
from half past the hour of eight in the morning, though
not to overcrowding as the admirable arrangements
made having prevented all crowding. The accommo-
dation for the press was considerably enlarged, but still
fully occupied and many hundreds waited outside to
compete for seats that might be made available.
The presiding judges were the Lord Justice McLennan,
Lord Arthur and Lord Thompson.
Elise Watkins, the prisoner, a young lady of short stat-
ure and slight build, with features sharp and prominent, and restless and shining eye, stepped up the stair
to the dock with all the buoyancy with which she may
have entered the box of a theatre. During the whole of
the day she maintained an unmoved appearance, her*

healthful complexion evincing how little, outwardly at least, she had suffered by the horror of her situation. Her head never sank for a moment; she even smiled on occasion with the grace of a young woman in the drawing room. She was dressed both simply and elegantly. She wore a blue silk dress, with a cloak of the same colour.

The indictment charged her with intent to murder, as also with murder and set forth that on the 14th of August last, in the house in Mansionhouse Road, Glasgow, occupied by David Maitland, did wickedly and feloniously administer to Sarah Maitland, now deceased, and then residing with her father, a quantity or quantities of deadly strychnine or other poison, to the prosecutor unknown, in sherry, or some other article of food or drink, with the intent to murder the said deceased; and that she having taken the said deadly strychnine, so administered, did, in consequence thereof, and immediately or soon thereafter, suffer severe illness, and on the 14th of August died, and was thus murdered by the prisoner.

The prisoner pleaded "Not Guilty" in an audible though subdued manner.

There was then a section where the reporter noted that Watkins *'fixed her penetrating gaze from the gentlemen of the long robe and the witnesses, as questions were asked and answered.'* Witnesses included the doctors Kenneth and Douglas who gave their medical opinion. Miss Watkins's landlady, the wife of a biologist, told the court that Watkins had asked her if her husband had any books on control of pests.

The reporter portrayed Watkins as having the coolness of a master criminal during the proceedings. Like a modern tabloid, there were great paragraphs about what she was wearing each day of the trial and a long description of how she looked. On the third day of the trial, Albert Reynolds, who was due to marry Sarah Maitland, took the stand. He told the court of his original betrothal to Watkins and how, when he met Sarah Maitland that he fell in love and called off the original engagement. He said that Watkins had been upset but reconciled herself to the new situation after a period of some months. Letters were read in the court showing the depths of Watkins initial anger at what had happened and the adjustment of her tone as she appeared to forgive the young man his change of heart.

The key to the eventual verdict was the prosecution's inability to find from where Watkins had sourced the poison, or to find any trace of it among her possessions. Not one witness could say for sure that they had seen the poison being added to the glass by the defendant. The reporter for the newspaper made his disgust at the verdict known. The final line of the report concerned the mystery of how Watkins might have obtained the poison.

> *The jury recognised the mystery, and without attempting to solve it, returned a verdict "not proven"*

Russell thought that with modern forensics, the young woman would probably have been found guilty. He struggled to think what this one hundred and thirty year-old case had to do with Michelle Armstrong. If the killer had used Strychnine where did they get it? Poison was frequently the weapon of choice for a lot of female killers. Could their killer be a woman? If so who?

He was convinced of one thing, he was now sure how Michelle Armstrong had been murdered; now he had to work out why and by whom.

*

When the detective superintendent had asked for the newspapers from August 1893 Tim Lauchlan knew that it was not a coincidence. Someone else had asked for the microfiche films for exactly that time period only a month ago. The killer had planned the murder of Michelle Armstrong in this very library, and now Tim Lauchlan had the chance to extort his way to some serious money. That cash would help to extricate him from under the suffocating attentions of his mother. The woman whose love had once been all encompassing now regarded her son as merely a source of income. She questioned every decision he made regarding his money and the only time she ever smiled was when he handed over his contribution to the household bills. He had grown to resent her to the point he could no longer stomach being in the same room, finally he would be able to pay the deposit on his own flat and begin his life anew. He began to make plans.

*

Alex's search through Kyle Allen's acquaintances had produced a veritable rogue's gallery of petty criminals. Every name on the list had a record, mainly for vandalism and petty drug offences. One name stood out, Jordan McDonnell. His list of charges stretched back nine years and included theft, drugs, house breaking and most significantly aggravated assault.

Alex called up the detailed file on that assault. McDonnell had broken the cheekbone and four ribs of a man who had accidentally spilled a drink on him in a pub. He had served nine months of a year-long sentence and had been released just two weeks before Michelle Armstrong's murder.

When she had taken note of his address, she logged out of the computer and headed for her car. McDonnell's flat was in Pollok and Alex was at his door within half an hour of leaving the station.

She rang the doorbell and was greeted by a fair-haired man in his early twenties whose eyes were fixed in a vacant glaze.

"My name is Detective Inspector Alex Menzies, I'm looking for Jordan McDonnell."

He replied, "Aw fuck, whit huv Ah supposed tae huv done noo?"

"As far as I know, nothing. I just want to ask you some questions about Kyle Allen."

"Ye better come in. Down tae the end o' the hall."

Alex followed his instruction and arrived in a sparsely furnished living room. There was a single armchair, a chair from a dining suite and a television perched precariously on a stand that was obviously too small for it. Alex caught the smell of cannabis in the air, which explained the glazed eyes.

McDonnell slouched into the armchair apparently unconcerned if she was there to ask him about his drug habit. Alex sat on the other chair without being asked.

"Make yirsel' at hame, why don't ye?" McDonnell said sarcastically.

His visitor ignored him. "I'm here to talk about Kyle Allen and in particular his death."

"Aye whit aboot it?"

"The woman who knocked him down and killed him has herself been murdered."

"So, whit's that got tae dae wi' me?"

"What was your reaction when you heard about his death?"

"Ah wis a bit pissed aff, he wis a mate but he wis also an arsehole. He just went mad oan the drink."

"You've not done too well on that score yourself."

"Aye, true enough," he acknowledged. "But somethin' bad wis always gonnae happen tae Kyle. There wis somethin' no right aboot him."

"Where were you on Friday night?"

"Here, and naw there wisnae anybody that can gie me an alibi. If you must know Ah wis huvin' a wee puff tae relax me. Ah've decided that me an' the bevvy don't mix. Ur ye gonnae arrest me fur it?"

Alex let the question go. "Are there any of Kyle's friends who might have wanted to avenge his death?"

He laughed, "Whit dae ye think this is the fuckin' Sopranos?"

"I was just wondering if there was somebody who took his death particularly hard, somebody who didn't think it was an accident."

He thought before answering, "The only wan might be his girlfriend. She wis a bit o' a bunny boiler when she wis wi' him. She wis really jealous o' any burd that spoke tae him. She went tae pieces efter he died."

"What's her name? His parents never mentioned her."

"Naw they widnae. He never tellt them and she never appeared at his funeral as she wis on diazepam or some shit tae keep her calm. Her name's Chloe Banks."

"Where does she live?"

"O'er in Baurheid. Ah'm no sure o' the address."

She stood up. "Thanks, you've been a big help."

"Nae problem, officer. Always willin' tae help the polis," he said, his face pulled into a grin.

"I'll see myself out."

McDonnell was either a world-class liar or was sincere in his attitude to his friend's death. Prison appeared to have taken some of the fight out of Jordan McDonnell, at least for now, how long that would last was another question.

At the car, she reached into her bag for her phone.

"Incident room, DC Hendry speaking."

"Graeme, can you get an address for me?"

"Yes, ma'am." She would have to speak to him about that term. She always felt like some aged spinster when she heard it. She gave him Chloe Banks name and the area that she lived in.

It took a few moments but eventually Hendry had found the address.

The drive to Chloe Banks's flat took her just ten minutes. She pulled up in front of a four-in-a-block house that had been painted a spectacularly lurid shade of green. Chloe Banks address was the flat on the bottom left of the four.

A tall man in his early fifties answered the door.

"I'd like to speak to Chloe Banks please," Alex said after showing him her warrant card.

"What?"

"I'd like to speak to Chloe."

"Do you lot never talk to each other?"

"I'm sorry?"

"Who is it Bill?" A woman's voice shouted from somewhere inside the house.

"It's a female police detective asking stupid bloody questions."

"For god's sake, man. Bring her in."

He stepped aside to let Alex walk in to the house. He showed her through to their living room, a room that could not have offered a more stark contrast to that of Jordan McDonnell. There was furniture all around the walls and the centre was dominated by a coffee table with Spanish-style tiles on top. Every surface that was available was covered with ceramic cats of every size, shape and colour. A large, real tortoiseshell cat occupied one cushion of the sofa, it raised a weary head to look at the visitor. Having decided that Alex was neither a threat nor likely to offer food, the cat went back to sleep.

'Have a seat, hen." The woman said. I'm Josie Banks and this is my husband, Bill. What was your name?"

"I'm DI Alex Menzies."

"Would you like a cup of tea or coffee?"

"No, I'm fine thanks." Alex was still puzzled as to what she had said that had offended Mr Banks so deeply.

"Now what is it you wanted to know?"

"I was hoping to speak to Chloe."

"I'm sorry you can't, you see Chloe passed away five months ago."

Alex felt like she was two feet tall. "Oh, I'm so sorry I didn't know."

"Obviously!" Bill said with disgust.

"Bill, the woman is just doing her job," his wife admonished.

"Not very well," he replied bitterly.

"I'm sorry Mr & Mrs Banks I had no idea. What happened?"

Mrs Banks said, "She died of a drug overdose. Heroin. It all started when she was about sixteen. She was never good at judging people but it got a lot worse when she started hanging out with a boy named Kyle Allen. He was a right bad bugger of a boy. God forgive me for a speaking ill of the dead."

"He was her boyfriend."

She sighed. "Not at first but she fell for him in a big way, then they were inseparable until he was killed in an accident. She was devastated."

"Imagine losing it over a scumbag like him," Mr Banks seemed to be holding on to a lot of rage that didn't seem to have a target, he was just angry at the universe.

Mrs Banks continued, "She left the house not long after he died. She stopped visiting, never telephoned and the next thing we heard was two of your lot at the door to tell us she was dead." The memory was clearly painful and Mrs Banks couldn't go on.

"I'm sorry for disturbing you. I didn't want to cause you further distress."

"Maybe check your facts before you come knocking on folk's front door." Mr Banks replied.

She left as quickly as dignity would allow. She drove back to the station exasperated by the fact that what little progress they had made was once more stalled.

CHAPTER 8

Ann-Marie Craigan was waiting for Russell when he arrived back in the office.

"Sir, Dr McNeill's been on the phone. The toxicology report is back and she wants you to give her a ring."

"Thanks Ann-Marie, is Alex back yet?"

"Not yet."

Russell tapped his mobile and rang the number for the pathologists at the mortuary.

"Can I speak to Doctor McNeill?" he asked.

"Can I say who is calling?"

"It's Tom Russell." He waited to be connected and then he heard Dr McNeill's voice on the line.

"Hi Tom, we've got some of the tox results back."

"Strychnine."

She was astonished. "Goodness me, how did you know that?"

He told her what he had discovered at the library.

When he was finished, the doctor said, "I've never seen it before, the only cases tend to be accidental; the poison not stored correctly that kind of thing. The asphyxiation that killed her comes as a result of the convulsions the poison brings on."

"How did the killer get her to take it? Wouldn't it have shown up in her stomach contents?"

"It's odourless, so it's impossible to detect during the PM. Strychnine affects the body almost instantly, so she couldn't have taken it during the meal. There was coffee in her stomach that was well sugared. Strychnine has a bitter taste, so the sugar was probably to neutralise that."

"Where would you get hold of it?"

"It used to be present in rodenticides, but it's been banned since 2006 in the UK. It's been replaced with compounds like Difenacoum and Bromadiolone. It's possible that the source was bought before the ban came into force and then left in someone's garage."

"Do you think it confirms your idea that the killer must have redressed her?"

"Definitely. Other symptoms include vomiting; spasms that begin on the face and spread throughout the body; as well as foaming at the mouth. I think the killer washed the traces away and therefore that he dressed her after she was dead rather than force her to put the costume on before he killed her."

"Anything else, Doc?"

"Just to say, you have to catch this guy. That poor girl would have taken two to three hours to die and she would have been in agony for much of it."

"Don't worry, doc. We'll do all that we can to put this bastard away."

When the call was over he relayed the forensic discoveries to the team including Alex who had walked in during the phone call. The details of what Michelle Armstrong had suffered were shocking. None of those present had ever investigated a murder by poison; it was something that seemed to belong to history. Now they faced the challenge of finding a callous killer who could watch another human being die in agony, and then calmly wash and redress them like a child's doll.

"This means we have to take this to the media, we can't continue to fob them off with excuses about investigations continuing. Usual rules apply; no one talks to the press except DI Menzies or myself. We don't want the details in the public domain, particularly the specific poison. The last thing we need is a spate of copycat murders. Do I make myself clear?"

The agreement was unanimous.

"Mr Hendry, any luck with the dress?"

"Eh…no, sir. Nothing at the costumiers, I'm still working my way through the vintage clothing shops and then I'll try the charities."

"Good stuff. The dress might have been lying in an attic but I think it's worth the effort to find where it came from. I know it is boring DC Hendry, but it is good and necessary police work, thank you."

The young detective looked immensely pleased and a little embarrassed. Alex was pleased to see that Russell was back to something like his old self. Every little positive sign meant she wanted to get to the root of what had brought about such a dramatic, sudden and pleasant change.

Russell continued, "Who's been looking at the CCTV?"

"That's me, sir," a uniformed constable raised his had.

"What's your name?"

"Morris, sir. Stuart Morris."

"What did you find constable Morris?"

"We can follow Ms Armstrong to the station, on to the train and pick her up at Partick but once she leaves the station the coverage is sketchy. The last we see her is in Dumbarton Road turning into Peel Street."

Russell continued, "That's a pain. Why is it the cameras are never where we need them. We've hit a bit of a brick wall, so we're going to have to widen the search. We need to dig into Ms Armstrong's life. She trusted her killer, so we need to look at friends; acquaintances; customers, basically anyone that she knew well enough to accept a cup of coffee from. I'll speak to Superintendent Carmichael and the ACC to see if we can get some more resources. Have we still got the victim's computer?"

"Yes, sir," DS Craigan replied.

"Let's see if we can compile a list to interview from her contacts. When you've done that, split it up and get a few folk ringing round and see if anybody can tell us anything helpful."

"Will do."

"Alex how did you get on with the friends of Kyle Allen?"

"Another dead end I'm afraid." She told them about her visit to McDonnell and the Banks family.

"Crap." Russell said. "I was hopeful that there might be something there. There's probably not much more we can do today. Fresh start tomorrow and let's hope it brings some progress."

Over the next half an hour the detectives finished what they were doing and one by one drifted away.

Russell was once again the last one in the office. He didn't want to go back to the flat but neither did he want to see Catriona Carmichael. The doubts about what had happened had begun to creep in during the day and he was now unsure how to proceed. She was an intelligent and insightful woman with a strength of character that would give him someone to lean on, but his male pride and the old demon guilt were eating away at him, refusing to allow him the possibility that she might even begin to heal him. He wasn't sure he was ready to let that happen.

His final act of the day was to call Assistant Chief Constable Lewis Baxter. The ACC was another reason that Russell was considering his future. With little front line experience, Baxter was programmed to be a manager and often failed to understand the problems that his officers on the ground were faced with. Morale had been low for a while, and was being made worse by the continuing cuts in the budget plus the demands of meeting performance targets. Cops didn't like the fact that some criminals were facing less serious charges simply so the force could meet politically motivated targets. Baxter was only interested in stats and budgets, managing the people in a sympathetic way didn't even cross his mind.

"Superintendent Russell," Baxter's refined voice said.

"Sir,"

"What's the latest?"

Russell briefed him as succinctly as he could.

"So you have next to nothing?"

"Just about."

"You realise we are on the clock with this. We can't have this hanging over us when the Ryder Cup starts. We don't want our visitors frightened to come to the city."

"I'll try to keep that in mind, sir. I'll make sure the team know how important is to catch this killer, so we don't scare away the tourists."

Russell's sarcasm flew over Baxter's head like a sprung grouse. "Excellent. Have you organised the press briefing yet?"

"My next call, sir."

"I'll let you get on with it. Don't forget that written report by the end of the day."

"Yes, sir." Russell returned the handset to the table and said, "Why don't you write down what I tell you, you knob?"

"Friend of yours?" Catriona Carmichael asked as she approached his desk.

"Our glorious leader."

"I thought it might be." She cracked a knowing smile. She knew that dealing with the ACC brought significant frustrations and challenges, she'd had them frequently. "How have you been today?"

Russell considered his answer before saying, "Better, I think."

"Do you want to have dinner tonight?"

"No thanks, Catriona. I've got a press briefing to organise for tomorrow morning."

"Is that the only reason?"

He realised there was no point in lying as she could sense his reluctance. "No. I need some time to think."

A sad smile crossed her face and faded quickly. "I understand. I'll see you tomorrow. Good night."

"Good night, Catriona."

When she had gone, Russell contacted the press office to ask them to arrange the briefing for the following day. Helen Paterson, the police media officer, was keen to hear the details of what had happened but she understood that certain key aspects would have to be left out. She told Russell that she would send out a brief statement immediately and call the press conference for ten o'clock the following morning.

*

As the sun began to set over the sticky, humid city, Russell found himself walking through the heart of Glasgow. The streets felt like a gridle, the unseasonal heat they had absorbed during the day was being radiated back towards its source. He could feel his shirt clinging to him as he sweated, small streams of perspiration ran down his forehead and he had to wipe away the sweat from his eyes. He passed a church with doors open and he felt a sudden urge to go in.

Inside the thick-walled building the air was cool, protected by those same walls from the stifling conditions outside. The noise of the traffic, the pedestrians and buskers was muted as he entered and he felt it was both a physical and spiritual haven.

Russell was not a religious man but in the tranquility that the old kirk offered, he felt a sudden sense of relief from the tribulations of his life. He switched off his mobile phone and found a place in the pews to sit. The decor was Presbyterian minimalist; uncomfortable seats, a simple cross sitting on a communion table, and a pulpit stained to near black by over a hundred years of varnish. The only decoration was the burning bush carved into the front of the table, the symbol of the Church of Scotland. There were flowers in vases on the windowsills, filling the space with their fragrance, which was joined with the smell of beeswax furniture polish that had been used on the pews.

He closed his eyes, bowed his head and breathed deeply; the motions of prayer the same as those required for meditation. He tried to concentrate on his breathing but his mind would drift and he began to feel foolish. *What am I doing here?* became an internal mantra and whatever chance he had of working out the answer began to be lost in the repetitions of the question.

He opened his eyes and stood up when a voice from behind him said, "Can I help you?"

He turned to see a woman in her late forties looking quizzically at him. She was dressed in a clerical shirt, under a pale green cardigan, with a bright blue skirt. She was tall with a delicate face and exquisite complexion. She was like no minister Russell had ever met.

"Sorry, Reverend. I thought I might be able to work something out but I don't think I can."

She smiled, "Well, it's not just God I talk to."

He was embarrassed. "Eh… no, I'm not a religious person."

"That doesn't mean I can't help. I'm not picky."

"It wouldn't feel right, you have parishioners to look after," he said feeling embarrassed.

"I could give you a stock answer about how all the children of God are my flock, somehow I don't think that would impress you. What about I'm a human being who helps other troubled human beings? You look like a troubled man to me."

He wasn't sure what to say and she sensed his unease. "Why don't we go to the vestry for a cuppa? No wine or bread, I promise."

Her humour and kindness penetrated his reluctance and he nodded.

"I'll just lock up."

When the church was secure, she led him to a room to the right of the pulpit. It looked much like any other office with a desk, chairs, filing cabinets, shelves and rows of binders. The differences were the black and cyan robes draped over a coat hanger, and a picture of the now familiar burning bush symbol on the wall.

"Have a seat. Would you prefer tea or coffee?" the cleric asked.

"Tea, please."

When she had finished making the drinks she sat down with a contented sigh. "I'm Mairead."

"Tom."

"So Tom, can you tell me what brought a good atheist like yourself into my little church?"

He considered for a moment before saying, "I suppose I was looking for somewhere quiet. Somewhere that offered me a place to think."

"But it wasn't working."

"No, not really. My mind is too busy to allow me to think straight."

"Would you like to tell me what troubles you?"

The woman's warmth and generosity of spirit touched something in Russell and he said, "My ex-wife was murdered over a year ago."

"I'm sorry to hear that. I take it you still had strong feelings for her?"

"Yes."

For the second time in two days Russell then laid out the complete story of all that had happened. He told her about his marriage to Karen; the subsequent divorce; his own role in the Harlequin case; Karen's death and the aftermath.

During his story, Mairead sat with her hands cupped around her mug of tea, sipping from it and occasionally nodding her understanding, but she never interrupted him nor asked a question. When he finished, she sensed that there was something more, something he was holding back.

"I remember reading about the case. I understand your guilt about Karen's death but there's another level of guilt, something you've avoided telling me. Do you want to try telling me what it is now?"

He let a smile brush his lips. "Do you want to come and work for me, Mairead?"

"Would I be the good cop or the bad cop?"

"Oh definitely the good cop."

"Damn, I always wanted to be the bad cop," she replied with a girlish giggle.

Russell laughed. "Of course, you're right. I have a new layer of guilt." He told her about his night with Catriona, and his concern that he had betrayed Karen's memory.

He expected the minister to offer some form of rebuke but he was surprised when she said, "And what's wrong with wanting some companionship and friendship?"

"I don't know. Karen was so jealous when we were married. I just keep thinking she would be so angry with me."

"I know you don't believe it, but I believe Karen has moved to another plane. I'm sure she knows how hard you tried to save her life, how much you loved her and how much you have grieved for her. I know it's hard to understand when grief consumes you but you can't let it define who you are for the rest of your life. You have to find a way to move on, a way to start living your life to the full once again."

He stared at her, absorbing her words and while he acknowledged the wisdom of them, he wondered how he could act on them.

"Thank you. I better go. Thanks for the tea."

"You're welcome to pop in for another one anytime. I might even manage some chocolate digestives next time."

"I might take you up on that. Thanks again." He left the solace of the church and headed home feeling a little better. The whisky bottle stayed in the cupboard and he managed a good night's rest without its help.

CHAPTER 9

When he returned to the office after the press conference, Alex thought that her boss appeared to be invig-
orated and more invested in a case than she had seen
in months.

When he had finished briefing the team - which amounted
to nothing more than a sharing of what little information the
detectives had gathered - he proposed that he and Alex should
go to talk to Janet Kerry.

"I was thinking last night that I had been blinded by Nick
Jackson, he seemed so obvious, but maybe this has more to do
with a jealous ex-boyfriend."

"Sounds like a possibility," she agreed.

"Janet's more likely to know about any problems than
Michelle's parents."

"True, I'd imagine that she would've probably have
confided in her friend rather than worry her parents."

"Let's go and have a chat."

They drove to the Cuppa Joe café in Kelvingrove Street, at
the west end of Sauchiehall Street. Decorated in an understated

combination of black and white, the café doubled as a lunchtime sandwich shop for the people who worked in a variety of small offices in the area. There was a counter at the back of the shop, four metal tables in the middle of the room, each with four chairs. At the window was a small bar with five longlegged stools facing out on to the street. As the two detectives entered the air smelled of coffee and pastries, and an Italian espresso machine hissed like an angry cat.

A woman was working behind the counter, Alex reckoned she'd be about the same age as Michelle Armstrong; her slim body was topped by a remarkably round face, a face that seemed to wear a permanently startled expression. Her drab brown hair was pulled back tightly and it bounced in a ponytail at the back of her head. Her green eyes were wide, bright and attentive, her smile fixed for customer interaction.

"What can I get you folks?" she asked pleasantly.

The two detectives showed their warrant cards as Russell performed the introductions.

"We'd like to speak to Janet Kerry, please."

"I'm sorry, she's away to the cash 'n' carry to get some stock."

"When will she be back?"

"She shouldn't be too long, half an hour maybe. Would you like something to drink while you wait?"

The detectives both ordered a coffee and sat down at one of the tables.

A short time later the woman came to their table with the drinks. "I take it this is about Michelle."

"Yes," Russell replied.

"That was terrible. She was a good friend of mine. I offered to help Janet out as this place was Michelle's pride and joy, and I don't want to see it close."

"That's kind. What's your name?"

"Yvonne, Yvonne Overton."

"And you knew Ms Armstrong well?"

"Yes, I met her a couple of years ago, we've been friends ever since."

"Do you know anything about her previous boyfriends?"

"A little."

She moved a chair as if she was going to sit down but at that moment a customer arrived. She served a man who was wearing a safety helmet and a high visibility vest. He ordered a sandwich and tea to take out, and when he was gone she returned to the table.

"We get a few builders in," she said as she sat down.

Alex began the interview. "Ms Overton, can you tell us a little about Michelle's relationships? Anyone she might have had problems with."

"What, like ex-boyfriends?"

"Yes."

She made a show of trying to think. Alex was immediately wary of her, there was something superficial about this woman that she didn't like.

"There was a guy called Fraser, Ben Fraser I think it was. She went out with him for a few months about a year back. He was a bit of an arse, really fancied himself. I don't think he was too happy when Michelle told him it was over. I think he was used to being the dumper rather than the dumpee, if you know what I mean?"

Russell nodded and asked, "Was there anything that made you think that he might want to hurt her?"

"He did this horrible thing on Facebook. Posted some pictures of her, 'photoshopped' so her face looked all distorted and grotesque."

"How did she react?"

"As far as I know she laughed it off, she thought he was a child basically."

Alex pressed the point, "She didn't feel threatened by it?"

"No, I don't think so. She never let it show if she was."

The bell on the door rang to announce the arrival of another customer. She was a woman in her thirties, dressed in a conservative business suit, carrying an expensive hand-bag. Cream and navy designer shoes tapped on the tiles as she walked to the counter.

When she had placed her order, Alex heard her ask Yvonne, "Who are your visitors?"

The assistant told her.

The businesswoman turned to the detectives. "Absolutely awful, what happened to Michelle. I do hope you catch the terrible person that killed her."

"You knew Ms Armstrong?" Alex asked.

"I'm a bit of a regular here, as a matter of fact. I got to know her quite well as a result." Her voice was refined; it was clipped and she sounded as if there was a private education in her past. The tone indicated she was clearly used to speaking with some authority.

"Can I ask your name?"

"Can I ask yours?"

Alex could see Russell scowl at the challenge but he flashed his warrant card and said politely, "Detective Superintendent Russell and this is my colleague Detective Inspector Menzies."

"A detective superintendent. Michelle's murder must be very important." Condescension dripped from her mouth like water from a broken gutter.

"Every murder is important to us. Would you be kind enough to tell us your name?" Russell's voice was beginning to show signs of stress and Alex was worried that the stupid woman might push her boss to say something that would offend her starchy, self-important persona.

"Patricia, Patricia Lockhart."

"Do you think you have anything to add to our investigation that might help us to find Ms Armstrong's killer?"

"Oh no, no. I never pry into other people's lives," she looked askance, as if Russell had asked her if she took her clothes off for money.

"Well, don't let us hold you back. I'm sure you're a busy woman."

It was Lockhart's turn to show her annoyance. Alex didn't imagine she was a woman that was dismissed too often, and definitely not in the casual way Russell had just done.

"I'll bid you good day then."

Yvonne Overton was smiling as she came back to the table. "I don't think you made a friend, Superintendent Russell."

"I'll weep into my pillow tonight but I'm sure I'll get over it."

"She doesn't pry into other people's lives! Who's she trying to kid?" the café assistant said.

"Why?" Alex asked.

"She's the biggest gossip that comes into this place. I've heard Michelle and Janet laughing about her. She was always asking them about their personal lives, trying to be subtle about it but she's as subtle as a tank."

"Do you think she knows anything about the murder?"

The possibility raised a brief smile but she shook her head and said, "I wouldn't have thought so."

It was another fifteen minutes before a harassed Janet Kerry returned. She was carrying boxes of paper cups as she bustled into the café, her hair and clothes dishevelled. The sight of the two detectives just added to her already worried look.

Alex introduced Russell and the young woman replied that she would be with them in five minutes.

When she eventually sat beside them, carrying a cup of coffee and a pained expression, it was obvious that the death of her friend was still having an adverse effect on her.

"Have you any news?" she asked Russell hopefully.

"I'm sorry, but no. We're hoping you can help us." He went on to explain that they were looking deeper into Michelle's background. "We were hoping you can shed some light on former boyfriends, colleagues or even customers that may have had a grievance with her."

"I know it's probably what you hear a lot, but she was a nice person. I've been racking my brain but I don't know why anyone would want to hurt her."

"What about Ben Fraser?"

"How do you know about him?"

"Ms Overton told us." That brought a glance in her assistant's direction that indicated she was less than happy at Overton's lack of discretion. Alex thought that Kerry was probably feeling sensitive and a little over protective of the memory of her friend.

She brought her attention back to the detectives. "Ben is a bit self-centred, I never really liked him but I don't think that he could have hurt her."

Alex asked, "What about these photographs Ms Overton mentioned?"

"They were pretty horrible but he is just a spoiled brat whose toys have been taken away. It was pathetic really."

Russell said, "We'd like to see them and have a word with Mr Fraser. If you've got any details we'd be grateful."

"I'll e-mail you what I have."

"Thanks. Is there anyone else you can think of?"

"No, if I could, I would tell you, believe me" she said with conviction.

"We'll have a look at Mr Fraser and tell you if we make any progress."

"Thank you."

When the detectives were clear of the café, Alex said, "What do you think?"

"Sounds like this Fraser has a bit of an ego."

"Maybe someone told him that Michelle had a date and that was enough for him to crack."

"Could be. We're definitely going to have to put Mr Fraser in the spotlight."

*

Ben Fraser's house was situated in the middle of rolling farmland in Renfrewshire. It was a relatively modern bungalow with broad windows that would allow the owner a wonderful panoramic view of the surrounding countryside. There was a substantial garage, a well-maintained garden but no equipment or animals that would indicate that the Frasers were farmers.

Russell rang the front doorbell and a middle-aged woman answered, followed by a Golden Retriever whose tail thumped against the wall as it stood with tongue lolling while it assessed the new visitors.

"Away back to your bed Dilbert," she told the dog before saying hesitantly, "Hello, can I help you?"

Russell ran through the formalities and asked if they could talk to Ben Fraser.

Her brow furrowed as she asked, "Oh, I'm his mother, is there something wrong?"

"No, we would just like to speak to your son," Russell smiled to reassure her.

"He's in his office, it's at the back of the house. I'll take you to him."

She led them through the house and out to a garden that was even bigger than the flowerbeds at the front. At the far end of an expanse of lawn stood a wooden building that looked like a converted shed. She knocked on the door and the detectives heard a man's voice call from inside. "What is it mother?"

"Ben, it's the police they want to talk to you."

The door swung open and an athletic man in his mid-twenties filled the gap. His thick black hair was carefully styled. Sharp cheekbones, a strong jawline and glinting grey eyes combined to make him handsome, and Alex could see why he would be attractive to many women. He was dressed in a sky-blue cotton shirt, midnight-blue chinos, with boat shoes but no socks on his feet. A waft of lavish cologne drifted out with him.

"You better come in," he said and led the detectives into the single room. There was a desk under a window, with an iMac computer on top. A large, comfortable desk chair, a couple of filing cabinets, there were some bookshelves but it was the two mirrors on opposing walls that dominated the area. At the opposite end of the room from the desk was a low brown leather sofa, which Fraser indicated as he said, "Take a seat."

They sat on the sofa but it was too soft and they found themselves sinking into it. They moved forward in unison and perched on the edge of the cushions. Fraser rested against the desk, which meant he towered over them.

"Can you please take a seat, Mr Fraser?" Russell asked. It was framed as a question but Russell's voice left Fraser little option other than to do as he was told.

Before he pulled the chair into position, Fraser had a quick look in one of the mirrors. It was a vain gesture so reminiscent of Alex's former fiancé that she nearly laughed. *What did I ever see in Andrew?* she thought.

Russell said, "Mr Fraser we'd like to talk to you about your relationship with Michelle Armstrong."

"It finished a while ago, what about it?" he asked casually.

"You do know she was murdered on Friday night?"

"Of course. I read the newspapers." Russell may as well have asked him if he took milk in his tea for all the reaction he got from Fraser.

"Murdered Mr Fraser. We're detectives, why do you think we're here?"

"To ask me about my relationship with Michelle, at least that's what you said."

Alex wondered if he was being deliberately obtuse or was he incapable of connecting the dots.

"Mr Fraser, I don't think you understand the seriousness of why we are here. Where were you on Friday night?"

He turned to the computer and tapped on the keyboard. After a few moments and some clicks of the mouse, he consulted the calendar on his computer.

"I was at my hairdressers from six-thirty until eight, then I came home."

"We'll need the details of your hairdresser."

Fraser hesitated long enough that both detectives noticed. "Eh… alright." He handed Russell a note with the name and phone number.

"Thanks. Can anyone vouch for your whereabouts after eight o'clock?"

He paused once again, and then said, "No, my mother was staying at her friend's in Glasgow, they had been to some show or other."

"So you were here alone?"

"Dilbert was here but I doubt he's much of an alibi," he smiled at Alex as if she should be impressed by his dazzling repartee.

Russell stood up. "Do you find something funny, Mr Fraser?"

"No," he said in a defensive manner that showed the child was not far beneath the mask of the man.

"Tell us about your relationship with Michelle."

"We had a few laughs then she had the temerity to dump me. She obviously picked up on the vibes that I was about to dump her." He had no idea how pathetic he sounded, he lived in a little universe that he was the centre of, inhabited by only him and his over-inflated ego.

"Is that why you decided to post those pictures of her?"

"That was just a joke. My way of showing what she was really like inside. Ugly."

Alex interjected, "Why? Because she dumped you?"

"Yes," he replied without a hint of irony or self-awareness.

Russell took up the questioning once more. "So you were angry at her. No woman gets to dump the great Ben Fraser. Is that right?"

"Absolutely. She should've thought herself lucky."

Alex laughed in disbelief. Russell shook his head. "You were so angry you decided to teach her a lesson. She just ignored your pathetic Facebook tantrum, so you decided to kill her."

All of a sudden it was like he had been hit with a plank. "What?"

"Did you stalk her? Did your rage overwhelm you when you discovered she was going out with someone else?"

"You think I murdered her. I'm not sorry the stupid bitch is dead, but I didn't kill her."

Alex's patience with Fraser snapped. "She walked away from you and that's enough for you to be glad she's dead?" she shouted.

She didn't notice the stern warning glance that Russell cast in her direction.

"I didn't mean it like that. I don't care one way or the other. When she dumped me, it was her loss."

"Now I know why you still live with your mother," she replied contemptuously.

"What's that supposed to mean?"

Russell made a placating gesture with his hands. "Right, this is getting us nowhere. Would you be willing to come to the station and give us a DNA sample?"

"No. I've not done anything wrong. I'm not putting my DNA on record for you to use against me."

"We are legally obliged to destroy the sample if there is no match," Russell replied.

"So you say. I don't care, I'm not doing it." He crossed his arms defiantly.

"Don't go anywhere, Mr Fraser, we may be back." Russell walked out of the door. Alex leaned over and whispered into Fraser's ear, "Stay with your mammy, Ben. She's the only one apart from yourself that'll ever love you."

Her barb failed to hit its mark. "Do you want my number, detective? Would you like to see what you're missing?" He flashed his overly whitened teeth at her as if would be enough to make her change her opinion of him.

Alex slammed the door at her back leaving him and his ego to their love-in.

*

It took a simple phone call to confirm Fraser's alibi, although when pressed the hairdresser did admit that he was there for more than just a hairstyle. Apparently he liked to have make-up applied professionally before he had his haircut. At every visit he would sit and admire himself in the mirror while the stylist cut his hair. This caused a bit of hilarity in the office but Russell was sensitive to his officers judging people's lifestyle and quickly put an end to the laughter. A further check of CCTV saw Fraser's car leaving the city directly after the appointment.

As the case began to falter, Russell asked the team to expand the search. He requested that the CCTV analysis be broadened and that the financials of those who had already been questioned be investigated.

The ever-eager DC Hendry was the one to discover a significant piece of information.

Two days after Fraser had been questioned he rushed into Russell's office carrying a piece of paper.

"Can I help you DC Hendry?" Russell asked.

"Sir, I think I've found something. Jordan McDonnell's bank records show he withdrew money from a cash machine in Queen Street half an hour before Michelle Armstrong left Mr Jackson."

"Oh he did, did he? Get the lying wee shite in here pronto."

"Sir?"

"Go with a uniform and pick him up. You do remember how to do that don't you?"

Hendry was surprised at being handed this important duty but he jumped at the chance. "Yes, sir." He almost ran out the door.

Russell shook his head. The DC's enthusiasm would soon wane but for the moment it was almost infectious.

*

When Russell and Menzies arrived, Jordan McDonnell was sitting smugly in the interview room, his arms folded and legs crossed casually in front of him.

"Jordan, you're not very clever are you boy? It's not wise to tell us lies."

"Whit lies wid they be, Superintendent?"

The two detectives were used to the casual disregard that career criminals had for law enforcement but they both sensed something different in McDonnell's attitude. There had been no screams for a lawyer and no claims of harassment. He was unflustered; he projected a confidence that said he knew something they didn't.

"You told us that you were at home on the night of Michelle Armstrong's murder and here we find you visiting an ATM in Queen Street not half an hour before she was standing in that very street."

"Ah lent ma caird tae a mate."

Russell laughed. "That would be very generous of you but you forget that the cash machine is fitted with a camera, so we know that it was you." This wasn't strictly true as the recording from the camera hadn't been secured yet but Russell was confident that it would show McDonnell.

"Ye're right enough. It wis me. Slap the cuffs oan, Ah withdrew ma ain money fae ma ain bank." He grinned.

"You've got to admit for us it's more than a bit suspicious that you just happen to have been in the same street as the woman that killed your pal, just hours before she herself was killed."

"Mr Russell, Ah know Ah'm no' a candidate fur citizen o' the year but believe me, Ah'm nae killer."

"So tell us what you were doing in the city that night?"

"Ah cannae. Ah've been told no' tae tell anybody."

"What do you mean?"

"Look Ah cannae say. Ye'll find oot soon enough."

There was a knock on the door and the custody sergeant's head appeared. "Sir, DI Jenkins from the SCDEA wants to speak to you."

"Ye'll find oot noo." McDonnell said.

Russell suspended the interview and left the room.

Jenkins was waiting for him in the video room. He was the senior DI at the Scottish Crime and Drug Enforcement Agency. At only thirty-four he was one of the youngest DIs in the force and was a contemporary of Alex Menzies at the Tulliallan Police College. He wore a charcoal grey designer suit, white shirt and red tie. His constantly tanned face was pinched thin and he sported close-cropped brown hair. Russell had met him a few times before and he was never impressed. Jenkins's false bonhomie grated on Russell's nerves and he wasn't convinced that the detective was all show and no punch.

"What are you doing to me, Tam?" Jenkins asked. It was another thing that annoyed Russell, no one called him Tam and like many in the SCDEA, Jenkins thought who he worked for was more important than rank.

"That's Detective Superintendent Russell to you Detective Inspector. Now what the fuck are you on about?"

Jenkins was unaffected by the rebuke. He continued in the same tone. "What are you doing with Jordan McDonnell in custody?"

"Look Jenkins, either you respect the chain of command here or you can fuck off back to Gartcosh."

Russell's anger finally broke through the DI's confidence. "Sir, Jordan McDonnell is one of our confidential informants."

"I don't give a crap. He's a suspect in the murder of Michelle Armstrong. I think that takes precedence, don't you?"

"He didn't kill that girl. He was being debriefed by one of our officers at a pub until midnight on the night she was murdered."

"Shit. Why the fuck didn't he just tell us?"

"He's been told not to tell anybody. He's trying to work his way up the Wright organisation to get some dirt on Peter Wright Junior. You know how hard it is to get to that bastard. We believe that Wright's got his own band of friendly coppers across the city. McDonnell was told to trust no one, not even the police. We've got a problem because I heard on the radio that you'd taken someone into custody for the murder. You need to put this right."

"Fuck, fuck, fuck. Who the hell told the press?"

"Not my problem but you might just have blown six months work. If you'd come to us it could have been avoided."

"Look you arrogant prick, I've got an investigation to run. I can't go asking you lot if it's OK for me to interview every bloody suspect that we come across. I'll sort this." He stormed out of the room.

Alex knew before Russell opened his mouth that the meeting had not gone well.

He pointed to McDonnell. "You, beat it."

"Ah tellt ye." McDonnell said as he left.

"What a fuckin' mess," Russell said. He told Alex what had happened and how he now had the press pack to contend with. With the investigation drifting on there had been less coverage in the papers and on TV, but the announcement of a potential suspect would promote it to the front pages once more. The fact that McDonnell was not the killer would allow the journalists to question the competence of the investigation and the team.

"Do you want me to do the press conference?"

"No, it's fine Alex but if I find who told the press, they'll be staring at fuckin' traffic duty for the rest of their career."

When the conference had been arranged, Russell was irked further by a bawling out from the ACC. There was nothing the detective superintendent could say to disagree with Baxter's assessment. The case *was* a shambles and the team *were* lacking discipline but the accuracy of the ACCs words did not stop Russell resenting them.

CHAPTER 10

Russell did his best to quell the press impatience but the conference was a thoroughly hostile affair. Baxter had appeared at his side and offered a decent defence of the MIT investigation but Russell was under no illusion that if the heat was turned on the ACC, he would happily throw the detective superintendent on to the bonfire of public opinion.

They discovered that a neighbour of McDonnell had called the local evening newspaper to tell them about the petty criminal's arrest. The journalist's call to the desk sergeant at London Road had resulted in the experienced officer confirming that McDonnell had been taken in for questioning. The rest was press conjecture but they had then connected McDonnell to the investigation. Russell ensured that the neighbour received a visit warning her about the perils of perverting the course of justice and how that could end up in a visit to a prison cell. It was doubtful the scared woman would call the press ever again. The desk sergeant got a dressing down from Catriona Carmichael and the incident seemed to blow over with no damage done to the SCDEA's investigation.

Over the next few days the trail went cold and the frustrated detectives began to consider the possibility that Michelle Armstrong's killer may evade them.

As October wore on and the trees put on their autumnal cloak, Russell and Menzies were asked to investigate a murder in Stirling. The resources of the Forth Valley area of the East Command were stretched to the limit by the investigation into the rape and murder of an elderly woman in her rural home.

The house where the murder that Russell and Menzies were asked to investigate had occurred was in Raploch, a tough working-class area of the ancient city. A woman lay on a threadbare beige carpet, which had been turned a deep chestnut around her head as the result of the fatal blow. This was the latest in a number of attacks she had suffered at the hands of her partner. The house had an air of neglected poverty with worn furniture and decor that looked at least ten years old.

Alex could see a menacing darkness overcome her boss as he stood over the poor woman. She was emaciated, her bones prominent on her face, as if the process of being reduced to a skeleton had begun long before the mortal blow. Her eyes carried a heavy baggage of dark-grey circles, the weight of a life filled with daily stress and little joy. Her bare arms were tattooed in bruises in a rainbow of colours. Her hair had been home-dyed a brassy yellow colour with no discernible style. The look on her face was almost one of relief; her struggle to survive was over.

"What's the story?" Russell barked at the uniformed sergeant who had been one of the first two officers on the scene.

"Janette Martin, thirty-two. There's a history of domestic abuse that included three broken ribs, a broken arm and one concussion. Her partner, Michael Rafferty has a record for assault but no charges related to the abuse as she refused to testify against him."

"Any kids?"

"No, thankfully not."

"Where is the Rafferty creature?"

"He wasn't here when we arrived. We're checking his usual haunts."

"When he's found, I want to be told immediately. I'll be conducting the interview myself. Do you understand?"

"Yes, sir."

Alex was wary as she saw the fury and bitterness of the previous months return. Her hope that he was on the mend floated away like a falling leaf caught on the breeze. "I could talk to him," she offered.

"No. I'll deal with him," he said, leaving no doubt as to his intentions.

With a different forensic team and an unfamiliar pathologist, the crime scene felt unusually stilted with none of the usual chatter. The technicians and the doctor worked efficiently but there was no feeling of the cohesive team the two Glaswegian detectives were used to. While they were still watching the technicians collect evidence the sergeant came back into the room.

"Sir, we've got Rafferty. He's at the station in St. Ninian's Road."

"Good. Come on Alex, let's go put the fear of retribution into Mr Rafferty, there's nothing we can do here."

*

Like his spouse, Rafferty was as thin as a blade of grass. When the two detectives arrived he was sitting with his head slumped over his concave chest. When he looked up, they could see that he had been crying and had tried to drown his sorrows somewhere at the bottom of several glasses.

He had already informed the custody sergeant that there was no need to call a lawyer and that he was ready to talk.

Russell confirmed the fact for the tape and the other necessary details.

He began the interview with a growl. "A bit late for tears, Rafferty."

"Dae ye think Ah dinnae fuckin' ken that?" Rafferty returned with drunken anger. As he spoke the fumes of the pub, stale sweat and cheap cigarettes enveloped the detectives.

The proceedings had not started well and Alex decided to try to defuse the quickly escalating tension. "Why don't you tell us what happened, Michael?"

"Ah dinnae mean tae killer. She jist widnae shut up wae her fuckin' moanin'. Ah'd only been fur a couple o' pints an' she starts fuckin' naggin' aboot it bein' a waste o' money. It wis ma money, Ah could spend it how Ah wanted."

"Did you not think that maybe your partner needed money for food, you selfish little prick?" Russell seemed intent on provoking an argument.

"She hud her ain money fur the hoose."

Alex spoke again. "You were at the pub and came home, what happened then?"

"She jist starts fuckin' givin' it plenty." He performed a puppet gesture with his right hand before continuing, "Ah skelpt her wan and she stumbled but she wis still fuckin' shoutin' and Ah hit her again. She fell backwards and her heid hit the coffee table." He paused and tears bubbled at the edge of his eyes and his voice became quieter. "She wis jist so still, there wis nothin', not a twitch, no' even a breath. Ah knew Ah hud killed her."

"And then you thought it would be a good idea to just leave her and head to the pub again," Russell's contempt poured out of him.

"Ah panicked, ken? Ah didnae know whit tae dae."

"You could have phoned an ambulance, that would have been a start. You're a coward, Rafferty, like every other bully I've ever met. I'm going to make sure that the Fiscal tells the judge the full details of your record before sentencing. A long spell in the jail with some real hard men might teach you what it's like to be on the receiving end."

He stood up and as he turned away he said to Alex, "Take his statement and I'll go speak to the Fiscal."

*

It took a couple of hours to complete the formalities as Russell spent time briefing a junior detective about the interview and then waited to speak to the Fiscal. He pressed the importance of emphasising Rafferty's previous violent behaviour in the hope that, despite the man's confession, he would serve the maximum time the judge could impose.

As Russell drove them back towards Glasgow, Alex could sense that he had retreated into his protective shell of resentment once more.

"Are you OK?"

"Fine. Just sick of little pricks like Rafferty thinking they've got the right to knock their partner around like they're in a boxing gym. What is wrong with them?"

"Psychologists will tell you it's a lack of self-esteem. They've been told that they're useless their whole lives and the only way they can counter that is to use violence to show that they have power over someone. He was probably raised in an environment where hitting women was a regular occurrence."

"Or maybe he's just an evil wee shite who doesn't know when he's well off." All of Russell's personal rancour and disgust was obvious; his complicated feelings about what happened to Karen were back at the forefront of his mind.

"Maybe," Alex replied believing that it was better to let the subject rest rather than prod those negative feelings and allow them to take hold once more.

As the Armstrong case was on a hiatus, Russell and Menzies were once again based in their home station in Helen Street. Fifty minutes after leaving Stirling, Russell had parked his Vauxhall Insignia and they were back in the office.

Russell walked briskly to his own little room at the end of the corridor, while Alex joined the rest of the MIT in the main office. Before Alex could even get her coat off, Ann-Marie Craigan called to her. "Alex, we had a call about the Armstrong case. Some guy saying he wants to meet a senior officer but it's not to be the super. He claims to have important information."

"Did he sound genuine?"

"Hard to say but he left a number."

"Thanks Ann-Marie. What's his name?"

"Lauchlan. He said he met the boss at the library."

"Oh, right. The boss mentioned him. He was the talkative librarian that fancied himself as a bit of a detective. It might be nothing; the boss said he was a bit strange. Why didn't he want to speak to Superintendent Russell?"

"The super can be a bit scary sometimes, maybe he wanted a friendlier face. As we're not exactly drowning in leads, it might be worth a call."

"We definitely need something before this case gets any colder. I'll give him a ring, thanks."

"How did it go in Stirling?" Craigan asked.

"Spousal abuse that led to murder. Got the guy, and he confessed. I wish they were all that straightforward."

Once she had made herself a cup of tea, Alex dialled the number that the detective sergeant had given her.

"Hello?" Lauchlan sounded puzzled at the call from an unknown number.

"Mr Lauchlan, it's Detective Inspector Menzies, I work with Detective Superintendent Russell."

"Oh, hello Inspector."

"I believe you have some information for us."

"I know who killed Michelle Armstrong but I want to meet you in person," he said eagerly.

"Well, why don't we meet at your local station?"

"No, no. I can't be seen going into a police station."

"Why?"

"I can't risk it. I don't want the killer to know that it was me."

Inwardly, Alex sighed. She was convinced that Lauchlan was just one of the attention-seeking nutcases that flocked to murder investigations like bees to nectar. "Where would you like to meet?"

"Tomorrow at seven o'clock at the gates of the Lambhill cemetery."

"Mr Lauchlan, you do know that wasting police time can lead to charges of perverting the course of justice?"

"I'm not wasting your time. I live nearby but it'll be quiet there. I promise I have the information you need."

Alex thought it highly unlikely but she said, "OK, I'll be there with Detective Superintendent Russell. For your sake you better have something."

"No, please come alone in an unmarked car. I don't want anyone knowing that I'm talking to the police."

"Fine, I'll see you tomorrow."

She put down the handset of the phone.

"Nutter?" DS Craigan asked.

"Definitely, but if he's wasting my time he'll spend a few nights in the cells."

Russell was less than impressed when she told him about the call.

"Another lunatic. You're not going there alone. He might be the bloody killer for all we know. The cemetery thing is a bit worrying considering where Michelle Armstrong was found."

"He's probably harmless but you're right, I wasn't going to risk being alone with him."

"We'll get a team in position in the cemetery long before he arrives and I'll be there."

"If he tries anything, he'll be in for a pair of sore testicles," Alex said with humour that she wasn't really feeling. Russell's more realistic view of the possibilities had made her feel naive and nervous.

"We'll make sure nothing can happen," he said with a reassuring confidence.

*

When Alex arrived home, Noel was waiting for her. She could sense that something was wrong; his usual smile was gone and his face was grim.

"I wasn't expecting to see you tonight," she said and then kissed him.

"No, I need to talk to you." There was nothing of his natural light-hearted tone.

"What's up?"

"They've decided to reorganise the photographers again."

"Christ, it's only been a year since the last time."

"They need to save more money. There's only going to be two full-time forensic photographers for the whole country. One to cover the south and the other for Stirling northwards."

"What? How the hell is that going to work?"

"They'll only be called on for murders and other serious crimes. The rest will be done by the forensic teams."

"You said they."

"I think Nicky Driver through in Edinburgh will get one of the jobs as she's got seniority over me and the other job will probably be based in Perth."

"You don't know that's how it'll pan out."

"There's more to it, Alex. I don't know if I want to be pointing my lens at corpses any more. A guy I went to university with is running a project in Moss-side in Manchester. He's teaching kids from deprived backgrounds how to take photographs while trying to get them to engage with their communities. He's secured funding for another photographer for the next two years and he's asked me if I'd be interested. The money's not great but it would give me time to do some more creative work again."

"Oh, I see," Alex replied, her voice flat.

"I won't go if you'd prefer me to stay but I need a commitment from you, Alex. I can't go on in this weird limbo where we're not quite a real couple but it's more than friends with benefits."

It was the kind of ultimatum that she had been expecting from him for some time, but it was still considerably more final than she had imagined. Manchester was only three hours away but she knew that Noel's need for more from her meant that a long-distance relationship would be doomed before it even started.

"I'll need a little bit of time to think about it. I don't want to hold you back but I don't want to lose you," she said as she stepped in to hug him.

His strong arms engulfed her, but she felt a sudden distance between them and that he was already beginning to slip away. She could hardly blame him; he had been more than patient with her and she couldn't expect him to put his life on hold due to her feelings of anxiety and her deep-rooted trust issues.

When the hug was over, he asked about her day. She told him the depressing tale of Janette Martin and Michael Rafferty. She decided not to tell him about what lay ahead for her the following evening; she didn't want him thinking that she was trying to manipulate his feelings in any way.

They ate dinner together and he left soon after it was finished. When he had gone she cried a little then composed herself before phoning her parents. She kept the conversation light and when her mother asked how Noel was, she replied simply that he was fine. If she had been face-to-face with them her mother would have read the situation and expressed her concern but Alex's voice hadn't betrayed her and she would bide her time before giving them her bad news.

That night her sleep was disturbed by the memory of arriving home to find her fiancé in bed with another woman, the root of all her insecurities haunted her still. She knew that she would have to let Noel go, for both their sakes.

CHAPTER 11

Rain battered down from the Halloween night sky as the police team assembled at the entrance to Lambhill cemetery. Huge puddles had formed around the gates as a river of water pooled at a drain blocked by fallen leaves.

Tom Russell was standing under a golf umbrella, giving out final instructions to the small team he had assembled that were there to protect Alex should her meeting with the evasive Mr Lauchlan turn into something sinister. Agreement had been reached with the council to allow the police to leave the gates closed but unlocked - Russell would lock them at the end of the operation. The two senior detectives were joined by Anne-Marie Craigan, a detective constable called Jamieson - who at forty-two was quite old for his rank, and a sergeant called Driver who had volunteered to step out of uniform when Russell had asked who would like to be involved. Driver's motivation was the overtime money that would help to support the costs associated with the imminent arrival of unplanned but very welcome twins.

The detective superintendent pointed to the building where generations of cemetery keepers used to live. "Sergeant Driver, you and I will take position behind the house. DS Craigan and DC Jamieson you go down into that small clump of trees to the left of the gates. Once we're in position I want everyone to do a short radio test and then it's silence until Alex tells us otherwise. Is that clear?"

There was a ripple of nodding heads before they moved towards their assigned positions. Russell addressed Alex before he left her to her solitary watch. "If you see anything suspicious at all, don't hesitate, use the radio. If he appears and you feel threatened in any way use the phrase 'time is up.' Do you understand?"

"Yes, sir. We've already gone over this."

"Better safe than sorry, DI Menzies." He put a reassuring hand on her arm before leaving to follow the other detectives.

Alex wished she had opted for a larger umbrella as the rain continued to pound down on to the street and splash back to soak her shoes and the bottom of her jeans. She acknowledged Russell as he ran through the detectives' names in a roll call of radio testing.

She checked her watch frequently and as a result time seemed to be dragging. The steady rain had dampened the enthusiasm of any local children for wandering around the doors of the nearby houses. In recent years the American 'trick or treat' had replaced the traditional Scottish Halloween guising, but there were neither tricks nor treats in the deluge and the street was quiet. An occasional car trundled by at a snail's pace; the speed restricted on the narrow street by a combination of parked cars and traffic control humps in the centre of the road. Apart for the vehicles the only other noises were animal; a fox howling in the distance - it's voice reminiscent of an unhappy child. A pair of tawny owls carried on a courtship conversation across the breadth of the cemetery, their exchange only added to the Hammer horror atmosphere.

Seven o'clock came and went but there was no sign of Lauchlan.

At ten past seven, Alex muttered into the microphone hidden on her scarf, "He's not going to show, he's just wasting our time."

"Patience, Alex," Russell's voice said into her ear.

Five minutes later she spotted a man walking towards her.

"Man approaching," she said quietly.

Out of the gloom a dishevelled and very wet elderly man appeared into the cone of orange cast by the streetlight.

"It's not him," Alex said to the microphone before the new arrival said, "Aw right, hen?"

"I'm fine, thanks."

"Waitin' oan somebody, ur ye?"

"Aye, he's running a bit late."

"Aw pet, ye've no' been dissied, huv ye?" His reference was an old Glaswegian expression that meant a potential romantic partner had disappointed someone by not arriving for a date.

"No, it's nothing like that. He's just a friend."

"Well darling, seein' as it's Halloween, ah cin show ye a trick or two, and ye'll definitely be in furra treat." He cackled lasciviously.

Alex reached into her coat pocket and flashed her warrant card.

"I'm here on official business, so you better move on."

"Fuck, ye're the polis. Well, Ah've got tae tell ye, ye're better lookin' than any polis that ever lifted me, that's fur sure. Nae offence darlin', nae offence. Ah'll leave ye tae whatever it is ye're daein'."

Alex grinned as the ancient lothario shambled back into the darkness muttering, "fuckin' polis," to himself as he went.

Time continued to drag and as eight o'clock ticked round Russell said, "Looks like he's a no show. I think we'll pay him a visit tomorrow and charge him with wasting our time."

"Sorry, sir. I was hoping we'd get something," Alex replied.

"It was worth a try, anything to get this bloody case moving again."

After they had gathered once more at the entrance, Russell locked the gates of the cemetery and then they headed back to Helen Street, damp and despondent.

*

Doreen Carrick's main source of exercise was a walk with her black labrador, Daisy. She loved the time she spent with the dog, watching the seasons change on her regular route through the expanse of the graveyard. Some folk thought that it was a morbid place but the peace and tranquillity of the cemetery was the perfect antidote to the hectic demands of being a nursing sister.

The rain of the previous night had finally abated and the morning was bright with only the occasional cloud scudding across the sky. The wind had blown the trees nearly bare and the ground was covered in a golden overlay of discarded leaves. Daisy had been happily exploring various piles of leaves, pouncing at them with the playful joy of a puppy. The dog had ran far ahead of her owner and as Doreen approached

Daisy seemed to have taken a keen interest in one particularly large mound of leaves.

"Daisy, come away from there."

The Labrador continued to dig at the leaves with her front paws, her tail wagging ferociously as she enjoyed her private game. It was only as Doreen neared her pet that she noticed that there was something under the leaves. Daisy had succeeded in freeing an arm from nature's impromptu robe. Doreen gasped as she realised what it was. She grabbed the dog's collar and leaned over, brushed away the leaves from the face of a corpse, who in life had been called Tim Lauchlan.

*

The same old scene; white-suited and uniformed bodies radiated from one point in the landscape, their epicentre another stilled life. Once again the outer cordon was set at the cemetery gates. A thin corridor had been created on the path to the crematorium from the car park to allow the two scheduled funeral services to be completed while the police and scene of crime technicians went about their tasks.

Sean O'Reilly was carefully lifting each of the leaves that covered Lauchlan's body and placing them into an evidence bag. He didn't have much hope that they would hold any clues to the killer but procedure dictated that anything that had been in contact with the deceased needed to be collected, collated and analysed. Above his crouching form, Russell, Menzies and Dr Rajesh Gupta stood patiently. The process meant a slow revelation of the body like some indecent and tasteless striptease.

Tim Lauchlan was dressed like a 'Teddy Boy' from the late fifties. He was wearing a long, blue frock coat with velvet-trimmed collar, a white shirt with a bootlace tie, drainpipe trousers that matched the jacket and a pair of thick-soled blue suede shoes. His hair was styled in an appropriate quiff and his moustache had been waxed to produce points at either side.

"Elvis has left the building," Dr Gupta remarked with dark humour.

When O'Reilly had finished his task he said, "He's all yours, Doc."

The pathologist lifted his bag and bent over the corpse. Blood had been washed through the right side of his suit staining the collar and shoulder. Gupta gently brushed the hairs of Lauchlan's beard before declaring, "Looks like sharp-force trauma to the right-side of his neck."

"That the cause of death?"

Gupta's smile was visible in his eyes despite his mask. "Come on, Alex, you know I can't say that until I've got him on a table. All we can say is that he was stabbed while he was living."

At that moment Noel - weighed down by his equipment - joined the group. His muted greeting and lack of smile told Alex all she needed to know. He was hurting and she was to blame.

Russell sensed the tension between his DI and the photographer, and made a mental note to quiz her about it later.

"Good morning, Noel. Can you take a few shots of the body before I turn it over, please?" Gupta asked.

"Will do."

Noel ran off a number of shots from a variety of angles within minutes. When he was finished Gupta - aided by Sean

O'Reilly - gently turned Lauchlan on to his side. As O'Reilly held the body, Gupta peered more intently at the wound. Doesn't look like a knife, the entry wound is very narrow."

"Do you think this is the same killer as Michelle Armstrong?" Russell asked.

"That's your department, boss. I just tell you how it happened. For example, we won't know until we've completed the tests whether poison was involved."

Alex voiced her thoughts. "Could be that the killer got the dosage wrong and had to finish the job by stabbing him."

"Maybe," Russell conceded but there was an element of doubt in his voice. Had Lauchlan been redressed? Was there particular significance to the grave that had been chosen? A whole new set of problems might be about to arise. The only small comfort was if it were the same killer, a second body would bring new clues and might reignite the fading fire of the investigation.

His phone rang and he stepped away from the grave. He looked down at the display to see the name of the Procurator Fiscal written across it.

"Shit," he muttered to himself before accepting the call.

"Fiscal. Are you on your way?"

She was her usual curt self. "No, I wont be able to make it but I want an update please."

"The body of Tim Lauchlan was found this morning in Lambhill Cemetery by a woman called Doreen Carrick. Preliminary investigations show that he was stabbed in the neck."

"Who's Tim Lauchlan?" she asked abruptly.

As usual she managed to get under Russell's skin with consummate ease. "If you'd bother to read the reports that you insist I send you, you would know that he was the informant that we were due to meet last night at the self-same cemetery."

She ignored his tone. "Is it the same killer as the Armstrong woman?"

"Let me get my crystal ball out and I'll tell you."

"Don't make me call the assistant chief constable, Detective Superintendent. Now can I have a civil answer?"

Russell swallowed his retort before he said, "As yet the pathologist has not established a cause of death. There are obvious similarities between the two crime scenes but there are also differences."

"I want you to treat it as one investigation."

"That is what we plan to do!"

"Where will you be based?"

"We'll move to Maryhill station. We're more likely to get information relating to this latest murder. The well has run dry on Ms Armstrong's case."

"Fine. Let me know when the PM is." She rang off before Russell could reply. He took a breath and moved back towards the body.

"Who was that?"

"Cruella. She wants us to treat this as part of the same investigation as the Armstrong case. I don't know how I manage to put my trousers on in the morning without her fucking advice."

"You would have had to confirm it with her anyway," Alex said, trying to reduce Russell's ire.

"I know but why does she always have to be such a cow."

"What about the ACC does he know yet?"

"No, I'll ring him when we get to Maryhill station. I told her that we'd be running the investigation from there, as we'll need to co-ordinate door-to-door. It will hopefully give us some new impetus." He turned to Sean O'Reilly. "You need anything from us, Sean?"

"No, we've got it all in hand, Tom."

"You know where we are."

"We'll see you again soon, no doubt. Give us a shout about the PM, doc."

He turned to leave.

Noel was fiddling with his camera as Alex approached him. "See you later?" she asked.

"Maybe. I'll let you know."

She wondered if he would even bother. The pain written on his face was a tough thing to see but there was nothing she could say in that setting that would offer him any relief or comfort. She followed Russell to his car with her heart heavy.

*

Before he turned the ignition key, Russell said, "So what's the score with you and Noel?"

"It's nothing," Alex replied evasively.

"Remember, I'm a detective, Alex." He started the engine and began manoeuvring out of the car park towards the road.

She sighed. "He's thinking of moving to Manchester. There's another reorganisation of the photographers on the way and Noel reckons they might let him go. He's got a friend in Manchester that has offered him a job down there. He thinks it would be a good time to move on to take pictures of something other than crime scenes. He said he would stay if I agree to move in with him but I think he's ready to go, he doesn't want to continue the way things are."

"And you're not keen on the idea of moving in together?"

She shook her head. "No. I know it's stupid but I can't quite get Andrew's betrayal out of my mind. I couldn't go through that again."

"Noel's not Andrew."

"I know, but my worry is that I had no idea what Andrew was up to until that day. I wasn't much of a detective when it came to my love life. What if it happens again?"

"Do you love Noel?"

"Maybe."

"And you would need to be sure before you could make a commitment to him?"

"Exactly. I don't want to hold him back, particularly if he's going to be out of a job if he stays here."

Russell concentrated on driving for a short time before he asked, "Do you think he loves you?"

"I think so. That's what's making this more difficult. I don't want to hurt him."

"You have to do what's right for you now, not based on what may or may not happen. When I decided to divorce Karen it was what I needed to do at that moment. This past year that decision has tortured me but it was the one I needed to make at that time for my own peace of mind. That's the only advice I can offer."

"Thanks, I think I know how it's going to pan out."

They lapsed into silence until they arrived at Maryhill Station.

CHAPTER 12

An hour later a small team of detectives had assembled for the first briefing. Russell walked them through what little they knew about the latest killing and followed it up with a short review of Michelle Armstrong's murder. He pointed out the similarities and the differences. That provoked a discussion about whether it was the same killer or maybe someone who had read the newspapers and decided to make it look like the original crime. The opinion in the room was divided with some of the more experienced hands leaning towards the copycat theory.

Russell set about allocating tasks. Interviews with Lauchlan's family, friends and colleagues all needed to be conducted quickly.

Ann-Marie Craigan had been to see Lauchlan's mother to give her the bad news. As Russell was detailing the work, she said, "Sir, I think you should interview the victim's mother. When I went to tell her about his death there was something strange about her reaction and I can't quite put my finger on it."

"You think she could be involved?"

"No, not really but it wasn't the normal reaction of a grieving mother. She's a bit weird I suppose and maybe it's nothing, but I think your experience might pick up on something."

"Right, you and I will go speak to Mrs Lauchlan."

"It's not Lauchlan, sir. Her name is Myra Gillespie."

"OK, Ann-Marie thanks."

A youthful and enthusiastic DC volunteered for the job of discovering where the lives of Michelle Armstrong and Tim Lauchlan might have overlapped. Russell was happy to oblige him.

Alex said, "Sir, I'd like to take a look at the name on the gravestone. If there's a connection between the murders maybe Lauchlan's body was placed on the grave of someone who was murdered."

"I think I would prefer that it's a copycat but we have to explore every angle." The last thing he wanted was another crazed serial killer; the Soulseeker case had been harrowing for everyone involved and Russell could not stomach the thought of something similar happening again.

He finished the meeting with, "Everybody knows what's required, so get to it."

*

Myra Gillespie lived in Skirsa Street, which was within walking distance of the Lambhill Cemetery gates. The flat was in a block of tenements that were built in the post-war era.

The Gillespie flat was on the first floor. The bell chimed and when the door was opened it was filled with a man who was big in every proportion.

"I'm Detective Superintendent Russell, this is Detective Sergeant Craigan. We'd like to speak to Myra Gillespie."

"Yous better come in." The giant turned and walked away from them into the hall. Russell and Craigan followed the broad, lumbering expanse of back to where Myra Gillespie was sitting in her living room. The detectives were met by a blast of hot air as they entered; the gas fire was burning at its maximum despite the relatively mild conditions outside. The room was like a time capsule featuring pieces of furniture that preserved the decades. There was a fifties sideboard, a sixties coffee table, a seventies display unit and an eighties bookcase which was populated with DVDs and CDs. The black and red carpet was stained and burned in places by dropped cigarette ends. There was a feeling that nothing had changed in thirty years, and that the occupants had turned it into a museum dedicated to their past.

Tim Lauchlan's mother was in her early sixties, gaunt with grey hair and dark green eyes. She appeared to be suffering from some kind of dermal condition; her skin was dry and cracked, and in places was peeling from her pale face and bony arms. Dressed in a loose fitting sweatshirt and leggings, she looked like a child wearing her parent's clothes.

"Myra, this two ur fae the polis. They want tae talk tae ye aboot Tim, an' that."

"Ma sister used to go oot wi' a polis, well a special constable. It wis aboot the time that Bible John was killing lassies. The boy she was courtin', he used tae tell me aw aboot it. D'ye remember Bible John?" she asked Russell.

The superintendent cast a glance at Craigan before he replied, "It was a bit before my time."

"Aye, ah suppose it wid be. You're too young tae remember how scary it wis tae be a young lassie back then."

"Ms Gillespie, we'd like to talk to you about your son."

"Aye, another wan gone. They aw go eventually."

"Yes, we know and I'm sorry for your loss, but we need to talk to you. Can you tell us when was the last time you spoke to Tim?"

She looked to her companion. "Last night or wis it the night afore?"

"It wis last night, Myra," the big man said.

"Sorry, sir. Who are you?" Russell asked.

"Ah'm Tony. Ah'm Myra's brother." He looked to be a little bit younger than his sister. His layers of fat were covered by a checked shirt - marked in places by food stains - and a pair of cheap jeans. On his feet he wore a pair of lurid green soft sandals over grey socks with a hole where the big toe of his right foot was visible.

Russell directed his question to the man. "You were here last night?"

"Ah live here."

"I see. Can you tell us what happened?"

"Tim wis gaun tae a party. He didnae say where but he wis like that; jist did what he wanted withoot a thought fur us."

"Did he tell you that he had arranged to meet my colleague at the cemetery gates?"

He looked to his sister before he said, "Naw, he didnae mention it."

Russell was conscious of Craigan writing something in her notebook. She had spotted the lie just as easily as he had.

"Is that right Myra, did Tim not tell you about his meeting?"

The woman shifted uncomfortably in her seat. "He might have mentioned somethin' but he wis a dreamer. We didnae pay any heed tae half the nonsense he tellt us."

"Do you know what he wanted to tell my colleague?"

"Ah don't know. Some rubbish aboot a lassie that wis murdered, but he wis like Walter Mitty. Half the things he said were aw in his heid. A bit like ma auld ma afore she died. She wis seeing fairies and god knows whit."

"Weren't you worried when he didn't come home last night?"

"Naw, he wis aye stayin' wi' pals. Ma sister wis jist the same, stayin' oot wi men. She wis a dirty hoor Ah'll tell ye that fur nothin'. Offerin' her fanny tae any creepy wee chancer that gave her the eye." She finished vehemently, a long-held grievance obvious in her every word.

Russell tried to keep Gillespie's focus on more telling concerns. "It was common for Tim to stay away from home?"

"Aye, he wis hardly ever here this past wee while."

"Did Tim mention a problem with anyone recently? An argument maybe."

"Naw, he widnae tell me anythin'. Jist come in, eat his dinner and go back oot again. He wisnae a big wan fur talkin'. Ma Da wis like that an aw. Jist treated this hoose like a hotel, so he did."

"What about Tim's father? Were they close?"

"We don't talk aboot him. He's goat nothin' tae dae wi Tim."

"Is there anything you can tell us that might help us to find who would have wanted to hurt Tim?"

"Naw," the brother and sister said simultaneously. Tony Gillespie's denial was more emphatic than his sister's.

Russell realised that there was little point in pursuing the interview any further as the pair were either completely ignorant or being wilfully obstructive - in which case he would have to come at them from a different angle at a later date.

"Thanks for your time and once again, I'm sorry for your loss."

Myra Gillespie didn't acknowledge his sympathy but replied simply, "Cheerio." Tony led the detectives out and muttered his own farewell before closing firmly the door behind them.

As they stepped back out into the street Ann-Marie Craigan was eager to know what Russell thought. "I told you there was something strange about them."

"I don't think I've ever seen a reaction to the death of a child quite like that one."

"She doesn't seem to connect emotionally, it's as if it's happening to someone else."

"But you would expect at least one of them would be upset by Lauchlan's death."

"The brother lied a couple of times but I'm not sure why."

"Aye, he's not very good at it. Could be fear. He might have some idea what Tim was mixed up in and be worried for his own safety." Russell said although doubting his own words.

"Did you notice something else? Among the pictures on the sideboard, there wasn't a single photograph of Tim as a child."

Russell nodded in realisation. "You're right. Who doesn't have pictures of their children?"

"And do you know what else is weird, there are only two bedrooms."

"I suppose the two men might share or one sleeps on the couch. However, I think you're right, they are a strange family but whether it's got anything to do with Tim Lauchlan's murder is another thing. We'll need to look closely at their history when we get back to the station."

"Do you think this is related to Michelle Armstrong's murder?" Craigan asked, clearly sceptical of a link.

"We can't rule it out but there is a different feel to it. We'll know more by the time we get the PM results."

*

While Russell and Craigan were busy with the Gillespies, Alex Menzies had begun to investigate a possible connection to the grave where Lauchlan had been found.

She studied carefully the photographs that Noel had taken of the scene. The simple headstone was more recent than the one on which Michelle Armstrong had been placed. A Celtic cross adorned the top and the inscription read:

Joseph Keen

Born 8th January, 1941

Died 7th June, 1962

Our angel is now with the heavenly host.

Alex used the computer to look for more information about the death. There was a single page of results; she clicked on the first entry from the archives of the Glasgow Evening News - a paper that had disappeared from the city streets some time ago.

The article contained an all too familiar story of Glaswegian violence. The 'no mean city' tag was coined in the thirties when Glasgow became infamous for rival razor gangs who clashed on Glasgow Green on a weekly basis, leaving a trail of injured and dead. In the late fifties and early sixties those gangs had enjoyed a renaissance. Young men once more gathered to prove their manhood in the spirit of teenage rebellion that had swept across the country as a result of the arrival of American rock 'n' roll, and movies like 'Rebel Without a Cause'.

Joseph Keen was one of the victims of that period of savage, testosterone-fuelled brutality. He had been part of a huge clash between one gang from the north of the Clyde, the other from the south. Police estimated that over 120 young men were involved with weapons ranging from the traditional cutthroat razor and flick knives, to butcher's cleavers and a screwdriver. It was the latter that put an end to the life of Keen - Alex noted that the story revealed he lived in Cadder. It went on to give details of his background that included several run-ins with the law, and that the police knew of his gang connections. He was hardly the angel that his gravestone had so boldly proclaimed. The newspaper reported that the police were willing to grant immunity from prosecution for anyone who was involved in the fight, if they would come forward and identify Keen's killer.

When she was finished reading the original story, Alex scanned the remaining search results but from what she could see, the killer had remained unidentified. She took a note to contact the cold case unit to see if they had any further details.

Once again there was evidence to suggest that the killer of Tim Lauchlan had copied an old crime, and there was a possibility that the same person had killed both Michelle Armstrong and the librarian. The problem with that theory was the two very different methods that were used. Although it was a generalisation, it was true that poisoning was a crime associated with women, or men who didn't want to get too close to the their victim. The face-to-face intimate but visceral process of stabbing was almost always associated with men, women tended to use sharp weapons as a defensive measure rather than as a method to commit premeditated murder. If Lauchlan had been stabbed with a screwdriver, it would have taken a considerable amount of force to drive it into his neck. The inconsistencies troubled Alex and she hoped that the post mortem might help to reconcile the two similar but different deaths.

Her phone rang, demanding attention. The screen told her that it was the mortuary.

"DI Menzies."

"Hi Alex, it's Rajesh."

"I was just thinking about you."

"I'm honoured," he said playfully.

"Don't get too excited, I was wondering when you were going to organise the PM."

"I was just calling to let you know that we'll be ready about four o'clock, if you can get someone to make the formal identification."

"That's great, Rajesh. I'll get that organised and see you at four."

She wrote up a short summation of what she had discovered about the death of Joseph Keen. She was typing the last paragraph when Russell and Craigan stepped into the office.

"How did it go?" she asked when she had completed the input of the data.

"They're definitely not the normal nuclear family," Russell said.

DS Craigan observed, "They are just plain weird. You should have seen the mother, no tears, nothing, she hardly seemed sad, never mind like she was grieving."

"Let's just say that it was a visit that raised a lot of questions. How did you get on?"

"The man in the grave was killed in 1962 during a knife battle on Glasgow Green. He was stabbed in the neck with a screwdriver and he lived in Cadder."

"That's a lot of coincidences."

"Exactly but why would the same killer use two different methods?"

"Was Keen's murderer caught?"

"No one was ever convicted from what I could find on the web, but that doesn't mean there wasn't a conviction. I was going to check with the CCU to see if it was on their list."

"That's a good idea, although I don't know if will help us with these cases," Russell said.

DS Craigan asked, "Has the PM been arranged yet?"

"Oh, yes. It's at four o'clock if we can get a formal ID done before then."

Russell looked at his watch and remarked, "We better move then. Anne-Marie, get a DC and take the Gillespies to the mortuary. I'll meet you there at four."

"Yes, sir."

"Does Cruella know?"

Alex replied, "I'm not sure, sir. Dr Gupta never said."

Russell sighed. "I suppose I better call her."

"I'll take a trip out to the CCU and see what we've got on record about the Keen killing."

"Let me know how you get on."

"Will do."

*

Alex went through the same onerous security procedure to enter the Crime Campus but this time she was met by a detective sergeant who greeted her with a firm handshake. He was a thickset but muscular man in his late fifties with a head of thick grey hair, dressed in a brown suit, lurid orange shirt with a black and orange striped tie, which looked constrictive around his bull neck.

"Fred McLintock," he said as he pumped her hand vigorously.

"DI Alex Menzies. Thanks for helping me out."

"It's just me the day, Ah'm afraid. We're no' a big team and the bloody admin has to be done sometime. Ah pulled the short straw this weekend." He waved his hand to indicate the way to his office. "If ye'd like to follae me, Ah'll take ye tae oor wee den."

As they walked Alex asked, "How many are in the team?"

"There's me, DI Fraser, DC Hamilton and DC Martin. We get some of the auld retired yins in as consultants noo and again. There's nain o' us under forty-five, it's like a geriatric waiting room some days," he finished with a smile.

"You've certainly had some success," Alex prompted.

"Aye, we've done no' bad. We've managed a couple o' convictions fur high profile cases that have been unsolved fur a while, and loads o' others ur comin' alang nicely. It's amazing the difference that the advances in forensics huv made. Made oor joab a bit easier."

"I'm sure there's plenty of good old-fashioned police work as well."

"At oor age Inspector, it cin be nothin' but old-fashioned." He grinned once more.

When they reached the small office McLintock asked, "Dae ye fancy a wee coffee?"

"That would be great, thanks."

While he set about his task, Alex had a look around the room. There were three incident boards on one wall, each filled with photographs and documents. The first was related to a rape and murder in Edinburgh from 1979, the second a double killing on a farm in Perthshire in 1985 and the third the abduction and murder of a young man in Glasgow in 1991.

"You've got a big workload for such a small team," Alex said indicating the boards.

"We're kept busy but it's good work. There's nae pressure o' time like you guys huv. Gie's ye a chance tae think. The retired cops ur a big help 'cause a lot o' them worked the original cases, so they can shortcut a big chunk o' the legwork that we might huv had tae dae otherwise."

"Do they find it difficult to follow the modern rules of evidence and procedure?"

"They aw moan but they realise it's goat tae be done properly if we're gonnae get a conviction. Milk and sugar?" he asked as he finished pouring the water into the mugs.

"Just milk, please."

He brought the drinks to where Alex was sitting and pulled a chair from another desk. When he was seated he asked, "Whit cin Ah dae fur ye, Inspector?"

"Please call me Alex."

"Well Alex, whit cin the auld codgers unit dae fur ye?"

Alex explained her interest in the Keen case.

"Ye think this is a copycat?"

"There are similarities between the cases but it's the second copy of an old crime we've had in the past month."

"Dae ye think ye've goat a serial killer in the makin'?"

"I hope not. The Lauchlan case is brand new so we haven't established a connection as yet. The problem is there are significant differences between the two murders, almost as many differences as similarities."

"And whit dae ye hope tae learn fae the Keen case?"

"To be honest, I'm not sure. It's a bit of a fishing expedition. I've had a look at the computer records but they don't go back as far as 1962."

"Naw they don't, that's a problem we come across frequently. Welcome to oor world, Alex. Wance we're finished oor coffee, Ah'll take ye tae the dungeon, AKA the archives."

"Thanks."

While they finished the drinks Alex asked McLintock about his career. He'd spent his early years in uniform in rural stations dealing with the crimes that provoked the indignation of local newspaper editors but that never merited a column in a national. Petty theft, the occasional housebreaking and dealing with the village drunk was not the kind of policing he had dreamed of doing. When the chance of becoming detective had been offered to him he had jumped in with enthusiasm. He knew Tom Russell, as he had been part of the team that investigated the Harlequin's second spree in 2003.

"Why did you not go for promotion from DS?" Alex asked curious as to why a man as committed and highly regarded had not moved up to inspector.

"Ah'm no a manager Alex, and there's too much management involved when ye move up. Except if you're in MIT," he nodded.

"That's true. I've got Superintendent Russell to take that responsibility," she acknowledged with a smile.

"Ah'm a detective. There's nothin' better than workin' a case and finding the bastard that took a life or ruined wan. The CCU gie's me a chance tae hunt doon the wans that think they goat away wi' it. Knockin' oan the door and seein' their faces when they realise whit ye're there fur is priceless." His face lit up with a satisfied grin.

"I can imagine."

"Ur ye done?"

"Yes thanks."

"Come oan, we'll see if we kind find Mr Keen's file."

He led her to a lift and used his security card to operate it to take them to the basement. The archives occupied an enormous area beneath the main campus building. It contained not only cold cases but also boxes of evidence from convictions that had to be maintained due to the possibility of appeals. In order that the documents were preserved, the room was temperature and humidity controlled. When they reached the small office attached to the main area, McLintock accessed a computer terminal to pinpoint where the files from 1962 were stored.

"This way," he said indicating a row of huge cabinets. They were designed to slide on oiled runners to open up space between them. As the pair walked the lights flickered to life above them. "It's aw very high tech. Saves oan energy."

They had gone about twenty metres before he said, "This is the wan."

He glided the great metal shelves aside and walked into the newly created gap. He studied the labels until he found the one he was looking for. "Och, it wid be oan the tap shelf," he muttered as went in search of some steps to allow him to reach his target.

He lifted a brown cardboard box from its perch and passed it down to Alex who was waiting at the bottom of the steps. The box was marked with the insignia of the City Of Glasgow police force and had Keen's name, the date of the incident and a reference number.

The two detectives walked back towards the entrance where four tables each with a chair, were arranged in a square. They allowed files to be studied without leaving the repository. Alex placed the box on the table and opened it.

Inside was a comprehensive collection of statements and reports. There wasn't much in the way of physical evidence although the investigating officers had found the murder weapon.

"Do I need gloves?" she asked.

"Naw, Ah don't think we'll be looking at this wan. The perp's probably long deid."

She lifted the screwdriver from a brown paper evidence bag. It was about twelve inches long from the point to the base. There were small brown traces where the blade met the handle that Alex believed to be blood.

"Nasty way tae go," McLintock observed.

"You're not wrong."

Also inside the bag was a brief report on what had been found on the weapon. It was indeed blood and it was the same blood type as Joseph Keen but without DNA testing there had been no way to prove that it was indeed his. The document also recorded the fact that the handle had been wiped clean of fingerprints - the best forensic proof they had back in the sixties. Alex put the screwdriver and the report back into the bag and turned her attention to the witness reports.

"D'ye want a hand?"

"If you don't mind and you're not too busy that would be great."

"Ah'll dae oanythin' tae get away fae admin fur a wee while."

Alex gave him a bundle of files and placed the remainder on the desk in front of her. For the next hour they sat in silence with the exception of an occasional observation or question.

Alex reached wearily for her twentieth file. It was a witness statement and it immediately caught her eye. It was a report of a door-to-door background interview that had been conducted by a PC. Alex exhaustion disappeared in an instant. The address was in Skirsa Street and the interviewees name was Mary Gillespie.

CHAPTER 13

Anne-Marie Craigan was waiting for Russell in the post mortem suite when he arrived at five to four.

"How did the ID go?" he asked as he settled into a chair.

"I don't understand it, sir. There was no emotion. You know how traumatic these things normally are. It was like she was identifying a complete stranger, the brother was just the same. I can't get my head around it at all."

"Once we're finished here we need to work out what the hell was going on in that house."

The door opened and Jacqui Kerr walked in accompanied by the ACC.

Oh shit, who invited him? Russell thought but said, "Good afternoon, Fiscal; sir. I wasn't expecting to see you on a Saturday." As he spoke he nodded to each of them in turn.

"Thought I should pop in. Getting a bit concerned we might have a serial killer on our hands again."

"That might be a bit premature, sir."

"Nevertheless, one must take responsibility and a hands-on approach."

Russell thought that if only investigations could be done on a spreadsheet, the ACC would be the greatest detective in the world but replied, "Yes, sir."

Despite it being a Saturday, Baxter was in full uniform complete with braid and medal ribbons. Russell thought there might be enough colour on his boss's chest to fill a Dulux paint chart. How a man with so little experience of real policing could collect so many medals had always puzzled Russell. Did Scout badges warrant a ribbon?

Jacqui Kerr took a seat opposite Russell, facing away from the window that offered the visitors a view of the autopsy room. She also positioned herself so the CCTV screen was not in her eye line. She always looked a little green around the gills when she attended a PM. The only pleasure Russell ever had when he attended the mortuary suite was to see her squirm. She lifted her mobile phone from her bag, dialled a number and began a conversation, ignoring completely those around her.

"As ACC Baxter is here, there's officially no need for you to hang on Ann-Marie," Russell said.

"I'd rather stay, sir," she replied. Russell was relieved.

Eilidh McNeil and Rajesh Gupta arrived in the other room where the corpse of Tim Lauchlan was lying in the body bag he had been placed in at the scene.

"Good afternoon, everyone," Dr McNeill said with a sigh of fatigue. All she wanted to do was get home to her son but one last duty meant that it would be at least a couple of hours before she could see his cheeky grin looking up at her.

All bar Kerr replied to the greeting; she was still engrossed in her telephone conversation.

The PM continued in the same way as every other. The body was checked for trace evidence and was then washed. Dr McNeill recorded her findings from a visual inspection of the remains - which showed no sign of defensive wounds.

Russell was never a passive observer of a post mortem; he always questioned and expressed his thoughts about what the evidence might mean. As the doctor revealed that Lauchlan had failed to defend himself, the superintendent said, "He knew his killer or he was taken by surprise."

"It looks that way, yes," the doctor replied. She was a little more likely to offer an opinion in the scientific atmosphere of the autopsy suite than she was at a crime scene.

DS Craigan was taking her own notes and she wrote down Russell's thoughts.

Trace evidence was collected and the body washed carefully by the attending technician. Before she began the process of getting under Lauchlan's skin, the doctor used a tool to measure the depth of the wound on his neck.

"8.5 millimetres," she said for the benefit of the recording from which her report would come.

The Y-incision was next, and Russell could see a fine sweat appear on Jacqui Kerr's forehead as she listened to the doctor describe her actions.

The pathologist peeled the skin from the neck. "The wound has punctured the carotid artery and would have almost certainly been the cause of death," she reported with formal and professional calm.

"As we thought," Russell said.

The next stage was the removal and weighing of the internal organs. When it came to the lungs McNeill said, "There is no sign of asphyxiation. We'll need to test stomach contents but if poison was involved it didn't get time to act on the victim's respiratory system."

"Does that help Tom?" Baxter asked.

"No, sir. If anything it complicates things further."

"We will have to confirm that through tests on the stomach contents and histological tests of other organs," McNeill warned.

"Yes, Doc. I understand," Russell reassured her.

The contents of the victim's stomach were poured into a bowl. As she raced for the door the Procurator Fiscal said, "Please excuse me."

"You'd think she'd be used to it by now," Craigan said, trying to hide her smile.

In the PM suite the doctor said, "Last meal was fried potatoes and a mince pie. Judging by the rate of digestion, I'd say it was within two hours of his death." She took a big breath as she stood over the bowl.

"No distinctive smell that would indicate any poison. Full analysis will have to be completed to confirm that."

"Oh, this is interesting," Dr McNeill observed. She continued for the benefit of the recording, "Subject has a genetic anomaly. He has three kidneys, two are of normal size whilst the other is smaller and appears to be diseased. Full histology will be required on the extra organ. Dr Gupta can you please confirm?"

Gupta moved a little closer and peered into the abdominal cavity. "You're correct, doctor, the subject does indeed have three kidneys."

"An extra kidney?" the ACC exclaimed.

"Genetic?" Russell said at almost the same time.

"It's likely. There could have been a problem with cell division in utero. We'd need to do a study of his DNA to be sure."

"Have either of you ever seen this before?"

Both doctors indicated that the discovery was a first. Rajesh Gupta appeared to be delighted. "There might be a paper in this," he said with professional relish.

There was no other information of any value to the investigation and at quarter to six the examination was over.

"Thanks Doctor," Russell said.

"Yes, thanks Eilidh. Excellent work," Baxter said.

"Now if you don't mind, I'm going home to my wee one. I'll have the report for you tomorrow," she replied.

"That's fine. Good night, Doc." Russell said.

The police and the Fiscal went their separate ways. Russell was left feeling that the results had only muddied the already dark waters rather than shed any light on them.

*

When Alex Menzies read the name of the witness she surprised herself with a squeal of delight. "We've got a connection."

"Good, what is it?" McLintock asked.

"A Mary Gillespie was interviewed during a background check into Keen. Our victim's mother is also called Gillespie and lives in Skirsa Street, as did Keen apparently, just two closes away."

"Is it the same woman?"

"No, the victim's mother's name is Myra but Mary could be her mother or maybe an older sister."

"Sorry, Alex but Ah'm no' sure how that helps you."

"At the moment I'm not sure either but it gives us something to go at the Gillespies with. Superintendent Russell said there was something strange about the way Myra Gillespie and her brother behaved; he felt they were hiding something. It's a hell of a coincidence that the guy who lived two doors away was killed in the same way as Tim Lauchlan, and Lauchlan just happens to end up on Keen's grave."

"You're right but you know it canna be the same killer."

"What if the murder in the sixties was nothing to do with gangs? What if one of the Gillespies was involved? What if violence runs in the family?"

"It's a stretch but Ah suppose it's possible. How dis it connect tae Michelle Armstrong?"

Some of Alex's enthusiasm disappeared. "I have absolutely no idea."

"Work the case, follae the evidence. That's what we're taught."

"You're right. At least we've got something to work on."

Alex made photocopies of the witness statement even though the detail was irrelevant. Having a piece of paper in front of a suspect always appeared to back up any accusations that the police might make.

The two detectives continued to analyse the remaining files for another twenty minutes. When they were finished Alex thanked McLintock and apologised for keeping him back from his own work. He escorted her to the door and as she was leaving wished her well in the investigation.

Excited by what she had found she called Russell before leaving the car park. Russell agreed that what she had discovered may be significant and that they would pick it up in the morning. For his part, he told her what had been found at the autopsy. When the call was complete she drove home with hope that they had achieved a breakthrough. It wasn't until she reached her flat that she thought of Noel. He had left a voicemail saying that he wouldn't be over, and her bubble of optimism was burst in an instant.

*

Russell faced a different kind of problem when he arrived home. The flat was beginning to feel more like a cell with each passing day. In the wake of their night of intimacy, Catriona Carmichael had called and texted him a few times asking him to join her for a drink or a meal. He had made a variety of excuses, turning her down as politely as he could. After two weeks she had given up and he had not heard from her since.

His monastic existence gave him plenty of opportunity to reflect on where he was going. The case in Stirling had affected him badly; the senselessness of the woman's death and her partner's complete self-absorption had knocked him back on his heels and made him begin to doubt once more his choice of career. He knew some detectives were just worn down by the constant need to wade through the effluent of broken lives and the sewage of humanity. Some of the perpetrators were just evil scum who would have found some way to show their sociopathic tendencies no matter what stratum of society they had been born into. Others were victims of their own history, circumstances or environment. People who were told they were hopeless almost from the minute they could understand what it meant and had then gone on to prove correct their family, teachers and social workers. Russell didn't know which of the two types was the bigger drain on him, the drugs barons and their psychopathic enforcers, or the hopeless cases like Michael Rafferty. He knew that no matter how many he caught there would always be more floating to the surface that required his attention.

He was self-aware enough to know that the majority of his feelings emanated from the day he closed Karen's lifeless eyes, but he had begun to wonder if maybe the emotions ran deeper than that. Had he just reached a point in his life where his job was no longer enough to sustain him? He had few friends outwith his fellow officers. He had no interests, no hobbies and he rarely socialised since his divorce. All he had was the job and now it appeared that he was ready to withdraw from even that. If he did walk away, what was left? It was a thought that was plaguing him more and more.

CHAPTER 14

The morning briefing concentrated on the Gillespies. Alex noted Russell's muted delivery as he assigned the work details to the team. He seemed distracted as he asked them to gather as much information as they could about the mysterious brother and sister. Once the briefing was over he retreated into a private office to write a report for the ACC and the Fiscal.

DC Graeme Hendry had been tasked with looking more closely at Tim Lauchlan and his place within the peculiar Gillespie family unit. He sat at a laptop and called up the program that allowed him to access the General Register of Scotland database. He typed in Lauchlan's name and his date of birth. When the search was complete he received his first surprise as the victim's birth certificate showed that his mother was not Mary Gillespie. He had been born in Glasgow in 1976 to a John Lauchlan and his wife Marion. His father was listed as a joiner and his mother a seamstress. Hendry began to wonder how Lauchlan ended up with the Gillespies.

He looked at other records for any further information he could find about Lauchlan's real parents. It didn't take long to discover that Tim Lauchlan died in 1978 due to complications that resulted from a dose of the flu. He wanted to be sure that he hadn't missed something and spent another half an hour checking the records once again in case he had been careless or had misunderstood what he was reading. When his research produced the same result, he decided that he should let the detective superintendent know immediately. He was sure that it was a big development and bringing it to his superior's attention might bring him some recognition.

He walked the short distance to the office Russell was using and knocked gently on the door.

"Come in," Russell said gruffly.

Hendry did as he was told. DI Menzies was sitting opposite a stern-faced Russell. Hendry had a sudden thought that this maybe wasn't such a good idea. Maybe what he had discovered wasn't that vital that he needed to disturb his boss.

"Well, DC Hendry?"

"Eh…sir. It's Mr Lauchlan, sir. He's not Mary Gillespie's son and technically he is not even Tim Lauchlan."

"What?"

"The register of births says he was born to a couple called John and Marion Lauchlan and that he died in 1978."

"Are you sure that it's the same Tim Lauchlan?"

"Yes, sir. I checked the records twice. The only Tim Lauchlan to have been born on that date died two years later."

"Interesting."

The DC seemed to be hovering so Russell asked, "Anything else?"

"I also checked to see if maybe he had changed his name but I can find no record of Myra Gillespie ever having given birth," the younger man replied enthusiastically.

Russell looked at Alex and said, "Very interesting. The Gillespies become stranger by the minute."

He turned back to Hendry, "Good work, Graeme. See what else you can dig up. DI Menzies and I are going to have a talk with Myra and Tony Gillespie."

Hendry left the room wearing a large grin and bearing a renewed determination to help break the case.

In the office, Russell began making plans. "Alex, I want you to take Anne-Marie and a couple of uniforms and bring the Gillespies in for questioning."

"Separate cars?"

"Definitely. I want them kept apart. We need to remove Tony from his sister and see what that will get us."

"Will do."

Alex left him to contemplate what it meant; his mind was now preoccupied with thoughts of the Gillespies and how the new information affected the case. There was obviously a complicated story behind their history and their current circumstances, but Russell was completely at a loss to think how it all fitted together. It was not a feeling he was comfortable with.

*

Alex and DS Craigan were the first to arrive at the address in Skirsa Street - the marked car bearing the two constables was delayed by an accident in Maryhill Road.

The two detectives waited in Alex's beat-up VW Golf. The two women liked each other but they were both tense and quiet while they waited for the uniformed officers to arrive. Both were wondering quietly about what they were going to do. The case had so many disparate strands and none of them seemed to intersect. It was Ann-Marie Craigan who broke the silence and voiced what they had both been wondering.

"D'ye think that Tony Gillespie killed Lauchlan?"

Alex shrugged. "I don't know. I've never come across anything quite like this before."

"Could the victim have been Myra's lover?"

Alex's disgusted expression told Ann-Marie what she thought of that suggestion but she said, "Stranger things have happened, I suppose."

Alex's Airwave radio crackled, "PC Vernon to DI Menzies."

"Go ahead, constable,"

"We're on our way, ma'am. We've got another car to respond to the accident."

"Understood, constable."

'We'll be with you in five minutes."

The two detectives lapsed into silence once more while those five minutes ticked by.

The four police officers arrived at the door of the Gillespies' flat, Alex in the lead with Craigan at her side and the two younger cops behind them, looking imposing.

Tony Gillespie opened the door and before Alex could say a word, the big man tried to slam it in her face, but Alex was ready for him and placed her body in the doorway, taking the full force of the attempted slam on her shoulder.

"Naw, ye're no' takin' her." Gillespie shouted as the two PCs rushed past the two detectives into the hall. Gillespie aimed a swinging punch at one of the men but the constable had seen it coming and backed out of the arc of the punch that sailed on and connected with the side of Ann-Marie Craigan's head. Fortunately, much of the strength of the blow was gone by the time it arrived. It only served to enrage the Irish woman who moved deftly and decisively to grab the arm and push it behind his back.

Gillespie screamed as she worked his arm as far up his back as his bulk would allow.

"Other hand," she ordered while he complained that he was in agony.

"Other hand," she shouted again while applying a little more pressure to his right forearm.

He complied and she snapped her handcuffs on him.

"Don't you take her, she's done nothin' wrang," he screamed.

Alex replied calmly, "Mr Gillespie, if you had bothered to listen to me before you decided to swing punches, you would have realised that we simply wanted to interview you and your sister at the station. Now where is she?"

"Ye're no takin' her."

Alex was a little less calm when she said, "We only want to talk to her. No one is under arrest apart from you, and that is because you have just assaulted a police officer. I'll ask again, is your sister at home?"

Her question was answered when Myra Gillespie called from the other end of the hall. "Tony, whit's gaun oan?"

"Ms Gillespie, we'd like you to accompany us to the station to ask some questions we have about Tim."

"As she walked towards them, Myra noticed what had happened to her brother. "Whit ur ye daein' tae him?"

"Your brother has assaulted Detective Sergeant Craigan. That is a very serious offence, but I am willing to overlook it if you will come down to the station with us without any further disturbance."

"Naw, Myra don't go. Ye've no' done anythin' wrang."

"Shut up, Tony. Ye don't want any mair trouble." She turned to Alex, "Ah'll come wi' ye."

She disappeared into one of the bedrooms and returned wearing a grey coat and black scarf. The two constables led her brother away while Myra locked the flat door and accompanied the two women to Alex's car.

*

With the Gillespies finally delivered to the station, Russell called both Alex and DS Craigan into his office.

He directed his questions to his DI. "How do you think we should proceed? Do you want to interview one and I'll do the other?"

"I'd like you to sit in on both, sir. The brother is very anxious about something. He thought that we were there to take his sister away. I'm not even sure that this is about the murder but there's a feeling that he thinks we've discovered a secret."

"Ann-Marie?"

She nodded. "I think DI Menzies is correct, sir."

"Who should we talk to first?"

"The brother," both women said simultaneously.

"Let's get started then. Ann-Marie I want you to watch the video link and if anything occurs to you, get a message to us."

"Yes, sir."

The two senior detectives walked to the interview suite, while the detective sergeant made her way to the video room.

When Russell and Menzies walked in, Tony Gillespie was sitting with his head down, after his run in with the officers at the flat his hands were still restrained only now they were in front of him.

Russell asked, "Are you calm now, Mr Gillespie?"

Gillespie looked up. "Whit huv ye done wi' ma sister?"

"Your sister will be interviewed shortly. We would like to speak to you first. Are you going to remain calm and allow us to remove those handcuffs?"

"Aye,' he replied morosely.

"Constable please remove those from Mr Gillespie's wrists and then you can go."

With the interviewee's hands now free, the detectives settled into the chairs opposite the man who now looked both uncomfortable and edgy.

"Mr Gillespie, I have to warn you that assaulting a police officer is a very serious offence and if you want to avoid a spell in prison it's important that you are as honest with us as possible. Do you understand?"

"Ma Myra's no goin' tae jail, ye cannae take her away from me."

"At the moment it's you who will be leaving her, if you don't co-operate with us."

Gillespie's shoulders slumped. "Ah don't want tae go tae the jail either."

"Good. Now we need to know more about Tim. First of all, who is he?"

He seemed surprised by the question. "He's Myra's son."

"We know that's not true Mr Gillespie. We've checked the birth registry and there was only one Tim Lauchlan born on that day that was listed in the records and your sister was not his mother."

"She's still his ma," he said defensively.

"We have no record of your sister ever having had a baby. Did she adopt him?"

"Aye, aye, she adopted him." His reply was quick but unconvincing.

Russell sensed it. "You're not helping yourself or your sister if you don't tell us the truth. Who is Tim Lauchlan?"

"He's Myra's son," Gillespie shouted back and stood up.

Russell matched the gesture and said in an even but firm tone, "Unless you want to go back into handcuffs, I would suggest that you sit down and remain calm."

Gillespie settled his bulk back into his seat but he still looked both uneasy and heated.

Russell returned to his place at the table. "We are going to find out the truth sooner or later. It would be better if we heard it from you or your sister. I don't like my team wasting their time having to dig for information when someone can tell me the full story without any difficulty."

Gillespie's body and face became rigid as he said, "He is Myra's son."

"That's fine, we'll speak to your sister while you are being processed for the assault charge."

Russell pushed back his seat but a shout from Gillespie prevented him standing up, "Wait, Ah'll tell ye."

"Let's hear it."

"Ye'll no' put her away will ye?"

"That depends on what you have to say."

Gillespie's head drooped as he muttered, "He wisnae her wean."

"We had already guessed that," Russell replied, his patience beginning to be taxed.

"She fun' him."

"Found him? What do you mean she found him?"

"Somebody hud left him in a bag doon by the canal."

Russell looked at his colleague and read on her face the incredulity he was feeling. "You're telling us that she found a baby and decided to keep it rather than report it."

"Aye. She wanted her ain wean but Ah couldnae gie her wan. So when she found him, she thought it wis a sign fae God. That's whit she told me."

"I'm sorry. What did you say?"

"See, ah knew you'd no' unnerstaun."

"Mr Gillespie, are you telling me that you tried to father a baby with your sister?"

"Aye. So whit? We love each other."

Russell was caught between disbelief and disgust. "I need a moment to speak to DI Menzies." He left the interview room with Alex at his heels. They walked to the monitoring room.

"What the hell is going on here?" he said with exasperation to the two women.

Alex replied, "I have no idea. I suppose it's possible that she found him but why would she not give him her name?"

Ann-Marie Craigan was equally perturbed. "I suppose questions would have been asked if she had registered him without having medical advice."

"So why choose that name?" Russell asked trying to make sense of his own confusion.

"She had to call him something. What lies would she have had to tell to her friends, family and neighbours? I suppose if he had another name she could have said that the father was out of the picture but that Tim had been given his name." Alex suggested.

"And I still don't understand what connects this mess to Michelle Armstrong."

"Did we establish any link between the pair of them?" Craigan asked.

Russell sighed. "Not that I know of. I think we need to speak to Ms Gillespie."

Alex studied her boss. His brief period of optimism of the early autumn had gone as quickly as the leaves had turned, and once again he was a man who appeared not to have much love for what he did. The fact that they had failed to find who killed Michelle Armstrong was certainly a contributory factor. Lauchlan's murder was now adding to his sense of disheartenment and impotence. She could see that the chances of him walking away from the job, as well as the only friends he had, were growing once again. She followed him to where Myra Gillespie was waiting but there was more on her mind than just this case.

CHAPTER 15

Myra Gillespie's demeanour was much calmer than her brother's had been. She sat with her arms crossed and looked relaxed when the two detectives entered the room.

Russell decided to turn the tape recorder on. He announced the formalities for the benefit of the recording.

"Ms Gillespie, we've been speaking to your brother."

"How is he? Is he awright?"

"He's fine. We'd like you to tell us about Tim."

"Whit aboot him?

"Was he your son?"

"Of course he wis ma son. Dae ye think Ah wid let a stranger live in ma hoose? Dae ye think Ah'm saft or somethin'? That's whit everybody thinks. Ever since Ah wis wee they thought that Ah wis saft in the heid but Ah'm no, and don't you say that Ah um."

"No one is saying that. Your brother told me that you found Tim, that you decided to care for him and bring him up."

"Tony's no' the brightest. He disnae always know whit's goin' oan. He's always been like that, a bit simple. Ma Mammy used tae say that he wis last in line when the brains wur haunded oot. She loved him but she knew he wis never gonnae be a brain surgeon. He's…"

Russell interrupted her and tried to get her back to the subject at hand. "What do you mean he doesn't always know what is going on? What doesn't he know about Tim?"

For the first time she seemed discomfited and unsure about how to answer. "He disnae know the full story."

"What doesn't he know?"

"Your no' gonnae unnerstaun. Naebody unnerstauns."

"Try me."

"It's a private thing. It's nane o' your business."

"We're investigating a murder. That makes everything related to it my business." Russell said sternly.

"It's got nuthin' tae dae with the murder."

"How do you know? Do you know what happened to Tim?

"Stoap it," she barked. "Ah want tae speak tae a lawyer. They'll tell me if Ah need tae tell ye or no'."

Alex could see from her body language that Myra Gillespie was beginning to become distressed. She tried to calm her down using a soothing tone. "Myra, we want to know who killed your son. We want to find the person who took him from you. Surely you want to help us"

"Ah cannae talk tae ye. Ah want a lawyer." The final sentence was shouted passionately and defiantly.

"Interview suspended at 1:46pm." Russell said before storming out of the room.

Alex caught up with him in the office where he was making a cup of coffee.

"Do you want one?" he asked.

"Yes please."

Ann-Marie Craigan joined them and made herself a cup of tea.

Russell seemed to be a little less angry by the time the three of them settled at his desk with their drinks.

"Did she kill him?" were the first words out of the superintendent's mouth.

Alex replied, "Her reaction suggests it's a possibility."

DS Craigan wasn't so sure. "She's not the biggest woman in the world. Would she have the strength to have killed him with a screwdriver?"

Russell conceded the point. "Possibly not, but she knows something."

The group fell into a brief silence while they drank. Alex was the one to break it. "I know it's a horrible thought and might be a little far fetched but what if she did give birth and Tony was the father."

"Oh god, please no." Craigan said in disgust.

"What makes you say that?" Russell asked.

"The two of them seem incredibly close for brother and sister, and there are only two bedrooms in that flat. What if they were having sex, she got pregnant but hid it from him? She would have to come up with some reason for the baby being there. It would explain what she said about him not knowing what was going on."

"But surely other people would have known." Russell said.

"Not necessarily. She's quite slight, maybe the baby wasn't very big, she disguised the pregnancy with her clothes. It's been done before."

Russell rubbed his forehead. "I suppose it makes as much sense as the 'Moses in the bulrushes' story that they spun. It still comes back to what does it have to do with his murder and how could it possibly relate to what happened to Michelle Armstrong." He paused, trying to compose his thoughts on how to progress. "Give Sean a ring and get one of his techs down here to take DNA samples. At very least we can establish if she's his mother or not. Either way there will be a whole different set of questions to be answered. Ann-Marie get as many of the team together as you can at three o'clock and we'll see what else we can do."

"Yes, sir."

The two women set to their tasks and left Russell to type up the latest bizarre information to send to the ACC.

*

The detective sergeant had managed to assemble some fifteen detectives in the office by the time three o'clock ticked round.

Russell stood at the incident board looking tired and slightly morose. Once he had briefed out what had happened with the Gillespies he asked for reports.

Neil Garner, a detective sergeant with an unruly thatch of curly hair was the first to speak. Russell was not impressed by the younger man's dress. The jeans, casual shirt and loose tie irked the senior man but not enough that he could be bothered to tell him to smarten up. Garner read from a notepad. "Uniforms have been round the doors of a good proportion of the Gillespie's neighbours. Nobody saw anything on Friday night that was in anyway helpful."

"Was there anything about what they thought of the Gillespies?"

The DS nodded. "The general impression was that they were a bit weird. It was a word that came up in quite a few of the reports. No one we spoke to said that they were friends with the family."

"Anyone know of any trouble between the Gillespies and anyone else?"

"Nothing like that, sir. They seem to have kept themselves to themselves."

"What about around the cemetery? Did the door-to-door produce anything there?"

"Not much. One man reported a van close to the cemetery entrance. He remembered a part of the registration plate number. We're working on that to try to trace the owner but it might take some time."

"Keep them at it, DS Garner. You never know we might turn up something." Russell was trying to sound encouraging but his own feeling of helplessness was pervading the atmosphere and the team seemed to be losing hope.

"DCs Hendry and Meikeljohn, I want you to work up a full profile on Tim Lauchlan. Known associates, financials, mobiles, the works. I know you've done some of it already but I want a comprehensive report ready by first thing tomorrow morning. Anybody got anything else?"

Alex said, "The forensic technician's been in and taken the DNA samples. Ms Gillespie's lawyer is here. Do you want to interview her again?"

"No, there's no point until we get the DNA results back. That'll give us the clue as to how to tackle them the next time. Let the Gillespies go."

"Will do."

"Anything else?" When there was no reply he continued, "Get to it and we'll meet back here at nine tomorrow."

Another meeting over, Russell returned to his desk.

*

By six o'clock that evening the daily report had been sent to ACC Baxter and Russell was sitting in front of his laptop reading and replying to e-mails. The office was dark; the only light came from the one above his desk.

When the door at the end of the room opened the movement sensitive lights began to flicker on. Russell looked up to see Catriona Carmichael walking up the narrow corridor between the desks. He could feel his face flush as she approached.

"What are you doing here?" he asked abruptly to cover his embarrassment.

"It's nice to see you too, Tom," she replied sadly. "I was at a planning meeting and thought that you might be here."

He regretted his lack of manners. "Look, Catriona I'm…"

"No need to apologise. It is what it is. I just wanted to find out how you were doing."

"I'm OK," he said defensively.

"That's good. How is the case going?"

"It's not. There are similarities between Lauchlan's death and Michelle Arnstrong's but there are huge differences too. What's worse is we can't connect the two."

She began to quiz him on the evidence that had been gathered so far and he told her about the confusion about who Tim Lauchlan was and where he came from. It was a cordial but strictly professional conversation and the awkwardness was only masked not removed.

"I'm sure you'll catch a break soon," she said. "I suppose I need to get home."

Russell had no idea how to even begin talking about what had happened between them. He had been rude and ungracious in his treatment of a woman who had only shown him kindness, friendship and humanity. Instead of trying to address his feelings of remorse and shame about the events at her flat, he said simply, "OK, I'll maybe catch you later."

"Aye, Tom, I'm sure you will." She looked crestfallen as she turned and walked away. Russell stared at her retreating back and cursed his own stupidity. His mood only darkened as the evening wore on and when he left the empty office at seven o'clock he was filled with self-loathing.

*

He had just clicked his key fob to open the car door when his phone rang. He didn't recognise the number on the display and thought about ignoring it but instead tapped the green button to answer it.

"Hello, Detective Superintendent Tom Russell speaking."

"Good evening Superintendent. This is Pat McIlroy at Shotts Prison. I'm afraid there's been an incident involving your brother."

Russell's torpor disappeared in an instant. "What kind of incident?" he asked apprehensively.

"I'm afraid he was stabbed this afternoon."

"Is he all right?"

"He's been taken to Wishaw General. Our doctor thinks he should be OK but he did lose quite a lot of blood."

"Do you know what happened?"

"A dispute with one of the inmates got out of hand," McIlroy replied with caution.

"I'll talk to you later. Who is investigating the incident?"

"Detective Sergeant Derrick from Wishaw."

"I'll speak to him later. I need to go visit my brother."

"I'm sorry about this, Superintendent."

Russell hung up and got into the car and drove as quickly as the law would allow.

It took him forty-five minutes to drive to the hospital. He asked at the reception desk and after a few minutes was directed to the correct ward. Eddie Russell was in a four-bed room although he was the only patient. His brother flashed his warrant card at the constable who was guarding Eddie and asked for a few minutes.

When the PC had stepped out of the room Eddie managed a weak smile. "The things Ah huv tae dae tae get ye tae visit me." The pallor of his skin was highlighted by a sheen of sweat. He had a drip attached to his left arm; his right was handcuffed to the bed. Tom hadn't been able to bring himself to visit his brother in prison and it had been over eighteen months since Tom had seen him, in that time Eddie had lost weight and appeared to have diminished in other ways; some of the mischievous optimism he had always radiated had gone and with it the essence of who he was.

"What do the docs say?"

"I'm lucky tae be alive apparently. First bit o' luck Ah've hud in ages." His shadow smile appeared again but it was unnatural and forced.

"What happened? The prison officer said there was a dispute."

Eddie managed a faint laugh. "The only dispute wis me no wantin' tae be stabbed and somebody else who wanted to stab me."

"Who was it?"

"A bastard by the name o' Bryant."

"Tommy Bryant?"

"That's the wan."

"He's one of Wright's men."

"Aye."

"Does he know I'm your brother?"

"If he disnae he wis the oanly wan in the place."

"I'm sorry, Eddie."

"Dinnae be daft. It wisnae you that chibbed me."

"I'm the reason you ended up here."

"Naw you're no'. I put masel oan this road a while back."

"They'll have to transfer you now, won't they?"

"I was due to be moved in the next couple o' months. Ah've been a good boy so I was gonnae be moved in preparation fur ma parole hearing."

"That's good."

The two men spent the next half an hour catching up. Eddie's questions about Tom's own health and life were gently rebuffed with bland reassurances but Eddie could tell that not all was well with his older brother. When the conversation fizzled out, Tom wished his brother well and told him he would visit again the following night.

Russell then went in search of Eddie's doctor. He found her lounging on a chair at the nurses' station.

"I'm Eddie Russell's brother. Can I have a word, doctor?"

"Certainly." She guided him to an empty waiting room.

"He said he was lucky. How is he really?"

"His intestine was nicked by the knife or whatever it was. We had to operate to repair the damage. It could have been a lot worse but the main concern we have now is infection. He'll be on IV anti-biotics for a couple of days before we can let him go."

"Is he going to be OK?"

"Providing there is no serious infection, he should be fine."

"Thank you, doctor."

Russell walked back to his car, where he sat for ten minutes staring into the distance. Although Eddie's actions had led to his predicament, in the end he had admitted to something he hadn't done. Eddie had always conducted his life with no thought to consequences but for once it was his brother who had acted without forethought, and it had led to Eddie's incarceration. He had been trailed to Glasgow from London by a couple of Serbian thugs that he owed money to. The Serbians had been killed by one of Glasgow's own gang lords in a gesture of gratitude for Russell's work in finding the killer of the gangster's son. It was a mess that Eddie had willingly taken the fall for, claiming that he had acted in self-defence. Although Eddie had survived, seeing him lying pale and in pain, looking vulnerable, only added to Russell's mountain of self-reproach.

The older brother rang DS Derrick to get more details but the detective couldn't add much to what Russell already knew. The occupants of Shotts prison were keeping quiet on what they had seen. Peter Wright had long arms that could reach all the way into a cell and all of those who weren't already aligned with him knew just how dangerous that reach was.

Russell's drive home to his flat was completed in autopilot; he was turning the key in his door before he was once more conscious of his surroundings. He couldn't be bothered cooking, so he made a cheese and ham sandwich that he placed on his dining table alongside the bottle of whisky. He drank the first measure in a single gulp, allowing it to burn like it was a punishment. He was about to pour a second glass when he decided that eating the sandwich would be a better idea. By the time he had finished the snack, his need for the whisky had gone. All that was left was the despair he felt, his belief that he was a curse for anyone who got too close to him. He was glad that he had decided to keep Catriona at arms length; he didn't want anyone else to be sucked in to his vortex of misery.

CHAPTER 16

The chill of a misty morning did not bring a cool head. Russell had a target for his anger, Peter Wright Jr, the second-generation drug lord whose son had been murdered as part of a spree of revenge killings two years previously. It was the same case that had also claimed the life of Alan McGavigan, the son of Wright's rival, Malky McGavigan. It was the complicated relationships that had developed during that case that had resulted in Eddie Russell's trip to prison.

Peter Wright Jr. was infamous for a level of violence that terrorised neighbourhoods and ensured that he was feared across the city. Protected by bent lawyers and dodgy accountants he had remained untouchable as his empire of drugs, prostitution and loan-sharking had prospered.

There was a deep antipathy between Wright and Russell that transcended even the normal levels of hostility that existed between professional criminals and the police.

Russell was not the kind of man who was intimidated by the likes of Wright, and he was determined that what had happened to Eddie was not going to go unchallenged.

He rose that morning with a fire in his belly that burned stronger than the effects of the whisky of the previous night. His breakfast was a cold croissant and a glass of milk that he consumed quickly.

He rang Alex on the way to his car.

"Sir?" she said as she answered the phone, obviously puzzled at the early morning call.

"I'll be a bit late. Hold the briefing until I get there."

"Is everything OK?"

"It's a personal matter."

His tone tripped warnings for Alex. "Sir, are you sure everything's OK?"

"I'll speak to you later." He finished the call before she could quiz him any further.

Wright's illegal earnings were washed squeaky clean by a number of businesses that gave him a veneer of respectability. His favourite was the private taxi firm he ran from a garage in Possilpark, not far from his home. From there he controlled both his legal and illegal domains, and Russell guessed it was where he would find him.

The detective superintendent walked past the receptionist and stormed towards Wright's office before the young woman could even react to his arrival. Two ugly meatheads - who were Wright's constant guardians - sprang to their feet when the door banged open as Russell barged in.

"Don't even think about it, you pair of fuckwits or you'll be in cells so fast you'll think you're Usain Bolt." The two looked to their boss to save having to engage their brains. Wright held up a hand and the two backed off although they didn't sit down. Russell almost expected Wright to throw them a treat to show what clever boys they were.

"Detective Superintendent Russell. Ye seem tae be in a bit o' a hurry." Wright had two stock expressions, supercilious smirk or red-faced rage. It was the former with which he greeted the detective.

"Listen to me, Wright. You put the word out now that if anybody touches my brother again they'll have me to deal with. If one of your goons gets within two hundred yards of him, I'll have every fraud squad member and forensic accountant in the country crawling through your every fucking orifice. Do I make myself clear?"

"I huv nae idea whit you're talkin' aboot." Wright replied with feigned innocence.

"As you well know my brother was stabbed in Shotts Prison by Tommy Bryant. Now Bryant's thicker than shit in a neck of a bottle but not so thick that he wants to serve more time for no reason. So what did you promise him? More money for his family, or would a blowjob from one of your tarts be enough?"

"Ah huv literally nae idea whit you're oan aboot. Ah cannae be expected tae know whit runs through the heid o' every acquaintance ah've ever hud, noo can Ah?"

"Wright you're more full of shite than a chemical toilet at a music festival. I've warned you. If you don't listen and heed what I say, neither these two arseholes nor your full gang will stop me getting to you and believe me I don't give a damn about the consequences."

Before Wright could respond again, Russell turned and exited at much the same pace as he had arrived. He heard the sound of laughter at his back but resisted the pull to go back and do what he really wanted to. He wasn't sure he wanted to be a policeman but he wanted to walk away on his terms and not with a charge of assault hanging over him.

*

The adrenalin that had fuelled his rage sustained him on the journey but by the time he walked into the office it had burned out, and he felt exhausted down to his very bones. His head was pounding with a pain that had taken residence like an unwanted party guest that refused to leave long after their welcome had worn out. Before he spoke to Alex he grabbed a couple of paracetamol from a bottle in his desk that he hoped would at least deaden the squatter's effects.

His DI asked once more how he was feeling but he waved away her question and dismissed it as a headache.

The detectives - who had been waiting for his arrival for twenty minutes - began to congregate around the incident board.

"Alex can you lead the briefing, please?" Russell asked as he perched himself on the edge of the desk nearest to the board.

She began by reviewing the door-to-door enquiries but they were still proving to be unhelpful. Cadder was another area of the city where mistrust between the citizens and the police was strong. Other than some elderly people who seemed to want the company of a young police officer for a short time, no one had anything to say.

Next she turned her attention to the profile of Tim Lauchlan that had been requested the previous night.

DC Hendry came forward. "We had a look at his financials and found something that might be interesting. Once a week since Michelle Armstrong's murder, he deposited £300 in cash into his account. There's no history of it before the woman's murder. Every morning of the deposits, he made a call to a mobile number. The number wasn't listed with a contact name on his phone and the provider has confirmed that the number is a pay as you go SIM. The telephone company also confirmed that it hadn't been active since the murder, so we have no idea who it belonged to. It's the same pattern as with the money; he had never called the number prior to the murder."

Russell said, "Is there any indication that he called someone connected with the case before the murder?"

"Not on his mobile, sir."

"Thoughts?" Russell asked the group.

DS Neil Garner said, "Could he have committed the original murder on behalf of someone? They decided that they didn't want to pay his bill, so they bumped him off."

Alex Menzies offered an alternative theory. "He doesn't strike me as a contract killer somehow. What if he knew who had killed her and was blackmailing them? The best way out of blackmail is to get rid of the blackmailer."

Russell perked up. "That sounds plausible but have we established a connection between Lauchlan and Michelle Armstrong?"

Garner shook his head. "Not as yet."

"There has to be something that connects these two cases."

"Maybe her family will know or maybe even Janet Kerry," DS Craigan offered.

"That's a good idea. You take DC Hendry and talk to the Armstrongs, Alex we'll go speak to Janet Kerry. Any word on the DNA results?"

Hendry replied, "They should be available by the end of the day, sir."

The briefing ended and the team went back to their mundane tasks while the senior detectives set off to conduct their interviews.

*

Business was beginning to ramp up towards the lunchtime peak when Russell and Menzies arrived at Cuppa Joe. Janet Kerry and Yvonne Overton were busy serving a short queue of customers, their attention on the preparation and serving of food and drinks. When Kerry spotted the detectives she asked them to take a seat and if they would wait until she was free. They sat down close to the window.

They had been sitting for about five minutes when a loud voice said, "Mr Russell, whit ur ye daein' here?"

A muscular man in his late twenties was walking towards the table with a large grin on his face. He sported close-cropped hair and wore a tight T-shirt with a sportswear company logo across the chest. His muscular arms were decorated in a variety of tattoos. He offered his dragonhead-decorated hand to Russell who stood to greet him.

"Ye don't remember me, dae ye?"

Russell paused studying the enthusiastic face. "Gerry… Gerry Nicholson?"

"Ye remembered," he said as he pumped Russell's hand vigorously. "Ah wis hopin' Ah'd meet ye some day tae say thanks."

"Thanks. What for?"

"If it wisnae fur you, Ah'd no' be here the day."

Although Russell had remembered his name, he had no idea what the story was behind their meeting other than he had collared Nicholson for something or other.

"Ah suppose ye don't remember everybody that ye've arrested, eh?"

"I'm sorry, Gerry, no I don't."

"Ye caught me after Ah'd been selling some junk but ye pit a good word in fur me and Ah didnae go tae the jail. I was oan community service when Ah met a guy called Ronnie Banks. Ronnie ran a boxing gym and he asked me if Ah wanted tae go train wi' him. Ah goat pure hooked oan it so Ah did. He helped me with a college application, Ah went and earned ma HND, noo Ah'm a fitness coach at the gym acroass the road." He pointed to the entrance of a martial arts gym directly opposite the café.

"That's great, Gerry. I'm pleased for you."

"It's aw thanks tae you being wan o' the good guys. I appreciate it Mr Russell." His beaming smile returned.

"You're welcome, I'm glad it worked out for you."

Nicholson shook his hand again before going to the counter to collect his lunch order.

Alex said, "That's a success story. There's a man truly happy with his life by the look of him."

"Yes, it's a rare win. Good on him for making something good from a bad situation."

"He did it with your help and I'm sure he's not the only one that you've helped down through the years."

"Aye, I suppose you're right," he replied.

Alex wanted the sense of hopelessness that Russell had been experiencing to be replaced by the realisation that his career meant something, and that thoughts of stories just like that of Gerry Nicholson would be the catalyst. Before she could try to point out Russell's long line of accomplishments, Janet Kerry approached the table, rubbing her hands on a towel. When her hands were suitably dry, she laid the cloth over her shoulder.

"Have you found him? Have you caught Michelle's killer?"

"I'm afraid not, we're here on another matter."

The anticipation disappeared from her face in an instant; she reverted to the anguish and distress at the loss of her friend and her shoulders sank. "Oh, I see. What else could you want to talk to me about?"

"It's about this man," Alex said as she showed the woman her phone that sported a picture of Tim Lauchlan. "Do you know him?"

"Yes, he's a customer. He comes in a couple of times a week for his lunch. Has he got something to do with Michelle's death?"

"That's what we're trying to establish."

Russell said, "His name is Tim Lauchlan and he was murdered on Halloween night."

"Oh, I see."

"You didn't read about his murder in the newspapers?"

"I don't read the papers, they're too depressing."

"What can you tell us about him?"

"As I said, he came in every Tuesday and Thursday. He always ordered a tuna baguette and a bottle of cola. He seemed nice enough."

"Did he take any special interest in Michelle?"

She considered the question before answering. When she did reply there was a note of caution to it. "I got the impression that he liked to position himself in the queue so that Michelle would be the one to serve him. He'd let others go before him sometimes, until Michelle was available. I think he liked her but I think he was probably a bit shy."

"Did Michelle ever mention having met him or spoke to him away from the café?"

"No, I don't think so."

Alex then asked, "Did you get a feeling that he may have been obsessed with Michelle?"

"Obsessed, no. I just think he liked her."

"Was there any change in his behaviour in the run up to Michelle's murder?"

"No, always Tuesdays and Thursdays and always the same order."

"What about afterwards? Did he still come in?" Russell asked.

A realisation dawned across the woman's face. "Now that you say that, no he didn't. I haven't seen him since. Do you think he could have killed her?"

"We are just trying to establish the facts at the moment. It may just be a tragic coincidence. Do you have any more questions DI Menzies?"

Alex shook her head.

Russell said, "Thanks Janet. You've been a great help."

When they were back on the street on the way to the car, Russell asked, "What do you think?"

"We at least have a connection but I'm not sure what it means. Did he kill her and then someone else killed him in revenge? Did he kill her for money? I have absolutely no idea."

"If we suppose that he had a romantic interest in her, why would he kill her?"

"She wasn't interested, she spurned him and when she agreed to go out with Jackson, he lost it and killed her."

"But poison is hardly the weapon of choice for a sudden passion killing."

Alex sighed. "No, it's not. Every time we take a step forward in this case, ten new pathways open up."

They reached Russell's car and when they were on the road he continued the discussion. "Let's take a look at it from a different angle. Like you said earlier, say he knew who killed her and decided to blackmail whoever it was."

"It would explain the £300 in cash."

"He demands more money and seals his own fate as the killer decides to get rid of him."

"It certainly makes more sense than him as the killer."

"But why all the elaborate ritual? Why would you go the risk of being caught just to stage the bodies?"

Alex shrugged. "I honestly have no idea."

*

Craigan and Hendry's interview had proved to be a lot less fruitful. The DS reported that the Armstrong family didn't have a clue who Tim Lauchlan was.

"How are they?" Russell asked.

"They seem to be bearing up quite well. Michelle's body is finally being released for burial at the end of the week, so they've started to organise some of the funeral details. Mr Armstrong is throwing himself into it, I think as a way of avoiding having to think about the reality of it all."

"It's how we West of Scotland men cope," Russell said with a gloomy smile.

"Superintendent Russell," Detective Sergeant Garner shouted from the other end of the office.

Russell looked up.

"It's Sean O'Reilly on the phone. His team have the DNA results. Will I pass him over to you?"

Russell looked down at the phone on the nearest desk. "Extension treble 5."

He picked up the handset on the first ring. "Sean, what have you got for me?"

"I don't know what to say, Tom. These results can't be right but I've double and triple checked them."

"What do they tell you?"

"According to this there is a familial connection between Lauchlan's mother and father."

"What kind of connection?"

"They are siblings. His mother and father were Myra and Tony Gillespie."

CHAPTER 17

With a calm detachment Russell replied, "OK, thanks Sean."

O'Reilly was disappointed his news hadn't provoked a bigger response. "You don't seem too surprised."

Russell paused. "We thought it was a possibility. You're sure about the tests. There couldn't have been any cross contamination that would give you false results?"

"I can't be one hundred per cent sure, but I checked with the technician that collected the samples and he followed procedures. I trust him, he's one of my best people."

"What about Lauchlan's original sample?"

"That was processed long before the Gillespies' samples were taken. There's no chance that they could have affected his."

"I know you're right Sean but we need to double check this. A defence lawyer is going to cast doubt on your whole lab as the notion of siblings having sex will be unbelievable to most people on a jury and the lawyer is bound to play on that disbelief."

"You're not kidding. It's pretty incredible to me but I understand. We'll run the tests again."

"We'll get the Gillespies in again. Maybe they'll come clean and admit it but if not I'd like you to retrieve the new samples yourself."

"Maryhill?"

"Yes. I'll let you know if you're needed."

O'Reilly said, "You think you've seen everything in this job."

"I know." Russell lowered the handset slowly and took a deep breath.

"Did he say what I think he said?" Alex asked.

By way of an answer, Russell's voice boomed out over the length of the office. "Folks, can you please gather round."

The detectives and uniformed officers shuffled into a semi circle around their superintendent.

"Forensics has just confirmed that Tim Lauchlan was the son of Tony and Myra Gillespie."

The suspicions of the senior detectives had not been shared previously with the rest of the team. With Russell's statement there was an audible gasp from a good number of the company and one long-serving sergeant muttered, "Dirty bastards."

Russell waited for the buzz of shocked conversation to subside. "This may have nothing to do with Lauchlan's murder but we now have a very sensitive issue that cannot find its way into the press. Anyone in this room as much as breathes in the direction of a journalist and the only thing they'll be investigating is a new career. Do I make myself clear?"

There were no dissenting voices and once again a buzz of conversation filled the room.

Russell didn't wait for silence, he just said loudly, "We have no idea what this might mean for our case but it changes the dynamics. DI Menzies and I will interview the Gillespies and we'll take it from there. The rest of you continue to try to put together the details of Lauchlan's life. I want someone to check CCTV for the days that he deposited the money in his account. Check the cameras around the bank; maybe he met his killer somewhere close. Unless you hear otherwise, full briefing at nine tomorrow."

*

Another hour had passed by the time the Gillespies were once more ensconced in separate interview rooms. Russell had decided to interview Myra first. She had made an effort to look good having shed her skin of ugly leisure clothes and replaced them with an unseasonably summer dress; white with large purple and red flowers across it. She had teetered into the interview room on a pair of scruffy high heels carrying a bright blue handbag. She had obviously used rollers or a curling iron on her hair, which was now in tight coils that clung to her scalp. Her face had been decorated with a thick layer of make-up that had been applied in the manner of an eight year-old girl playing with her mother's lipstick and eyeliner. Beside her a young female lawyer looked very restrained in comparison.

Once Russell had completed the recording formalities he sat with his hands clasped in front of him on the interview table. "Myra we've had the results of your DNA test. Our technicians have analysed the samples and say that you are Tim's mother and that your brother is his father."

The young lawyer's surprise could not have been more obvious if she had jumped up from her chair and ran from the room. Her jaw fell as she gaped at her client before she tried to compose herself by fussing with her pen and notepad in an effort to regain some measure of professional calm.

For her part Myra Gillespie was unruffled. "I told ye he wis ma boy."

"Can you please tell us what happened?"

The woman stared at him, her face a study of passivity. The silence stretched on for over two minutes, Russell was happy to let it go on until she responded.

The other woman said, "Myra you don't need to answer that if you don't want to."

"Naw, Ah need tae tell them." She addressed Russell. "Ye'll no' believe me, naebody will."

"Try us."

"We wur always a close faemily. Ma da said that ma mother wisnae right in the heid. She wis scared o' everythin' and everybody. Me an' Tony wurnae allowed tae play wi any other weans, we wurnae allowed tae go oot unless it wis tae school and even then she sometimes kept us aff 'cause she wis scared somethin' wid happen tae us. Ma dad wis a drinker, in truth he couldnae take ma maw's type o' crazy and the drink wis his way o' dealin' wi' it. It got too much fur him and he left when we wur teenagers. Ma sister wis a lot aulder than us, she wis already livin' wi' her man in her ain hoose. It wis jist me and Tony, and ma crazy auld maw. Ah never hud a boyfriend, he never hud a girlfriend. We sherred a room and wan night efter ma mother hud wan o' her eppies; flingin' cups and plates aboot the place like a maddy, me and Tony jist huddled the gither in oor bedroom." She paused obviously disturbed by the memory of that night.

Russell prompted her to continue. "Is that when you first had sex?"

Her face contorted in anger. "That's the first time we made love." Her lawyer's complexion was now a pale shade of green and she looked like she might throw up. Alex doubted that all she had learned at university had prepared the solicitor for anything quite like this, but then with nearly fifty years of experience between them, nothing had prepared the two detectives for a story like this either.

Russell raised his hands in supplication. "I'm sorry, that was the first time you made love."

"We wur teenagers. We needed comfort." She said defiantly.

"Was Tim conceived that night?"

"Naw, naw. That wis years later."

"So your relationship continued. Did you make love regularly?"

"Aye." Her tone challenged him to condemn them.

"Did your mother know what was going on?"

"Naw. Stupid auld bitch didnae know whit day o' the week it wis half the time."

"Was she still living when Tim was born?"

"Naw, she passed the year afore."

Alex was curious about one aspect of the story. "Why does Tony think that you found Tim?"

"When ma maw died, Ah told him Ah wanted a room tae masel'. Ah knew Ah wis pregnant but as the months went by Ah didnae get much bigger. Ah knew if folk fun' oot whit we hud done, they widnae allow me tae keep the baby. That big eejit wid huv said somethin' tae somebody if he knew he wis the faither. Ah couldnae risk that."

Russell was struggling to follow her logic. "But surely you knew that people would ask questions about Tim."

"Aye, but Ah could tell them that his faither wis oot the picture, like it wis a wan night staun kind o' thing."

"Did you get medical attention at all?"

"Naw, well no' official. There wis a lassie in the same class as me at school whose ma was a midwife. She agreed tae help me when the time came. Ah gave birth in her hoose."

Alex asked, "Why would she do that?"

"Ah gave her money, told her that Ah wis embarrassed aboot whit hud happened and didnae want anybody else tae know."

"Did you tell the midwife who the father was?"

"Naw, jist the same story Ah tellt everybody else."

"What did you tell Tony when the time came to give birth?" Russell asked.

"Ah tellt him that Ah wis gaun away fur a couple o' days tae a pal's hoose. When Ah got back Ah said Ah hud fun' Tim at the canal."

"And he believed you?"

"Aye, as Ah said he's no' the brightest. He knew that Ah hudnae been wi' anybody else, so Ah hud tae come up wi' a story that he'd believe."

"What happened next?"

"We kept tae oorsel's. It wis hard 'cause folk wanted tae know aboot oor Tim but Ah stuck tae ma story. When it was getting close tae huvin' tae send Tim tae school, Ah wis walkin' through the cemetery wan day and Ah saw this gravestane wi' the name Tim Lauchlan oan it. When Ah realised that it wis a baby that hud been born the same year as oor wean, Ah hud an idea."

Alex guessed what that idea had been. "You registered your son as Tim Lauchlan at the school."

"Aye, it seemed an easy solution."

Russell continued, "What had you been calling him up until then?"

"Jim, same as ma auld granddad, so Tim didnae sound too different."

"Did Tim know who his real father was?"

"Naw, as far as he knew his Da was an Irish sailor."

"He never suspected the truth?"

"Naw."

"And Tony never told him that he had been found next to the canal?"

"Naw, Ah warned Tony that if Tim told an ootsider that he'd been fun', they'd take him away. Tony jist did as Ah told him."

"Do you know what happened to Tim at Halloween?"

She paused before answering, looking to her lawyer as for guidance.

"If you know somethin' it's better that you tell us now," Russell prompted.

"Aye, Ah know somethin'."

"So tell us what happened."

"It wis aw Tim's fault. He came in an' tellt us that he wis leavin'. He told us that he'd found a way tae make some extra money and that he wis gonnae get his ain hoose. Tony an' him argued, Tony loast the plot and got a screwdriver oot the drawer and stabbed him in the neck." She delivered the whole tale dispassionately as if reciting a grocery list.

"Tony killed him?" Russell asked for confirmation.

"Aye."

"Did Tim tell you where this extra money was going to come from?"

"He said it wis somethin' tae dae wi' the lassie that died but he didnae say exactly where the money was coming fae."

"How did Tim end up in the graveyard?"

"Tony wis panickin', 'Whit Ah'm ah gonnae dae? The polis will take me away fae ye.' Ah told him tae calm doon. Ah hud an idea. Ah remembered aboot the guy who had been stabbed in the neck back in the sixties. Ma mother wis questioned by the polis back then aboot him. She told me aw aboot it. Ah knew he wis buried in Lambhill Cemetery. Ah thought if we put him oan the grave, youse wid think it wis the same person that hud killed that lassie."

"Do you think Tim had something to do with Michelle Armstrong's murder?"

She shook her head, "Naw, nae chance o' that." Her denial was vehement and absolute.

Russell did well to hide his disappointment as his hope of clearing up both cases in one interview disappeared.

"We're going to speak to your brother. Will he tell us the same story?"

"Ah don't know but that's whit happened."

"Interview suspended at three fourteen." He pressed stop on the recorder and then said, "Thanks for your help, Ms Gillespie. We may have a few more questions."

"Aye fine."

Russell and Menzies left the interview room, leaving a serene Gillespie and a lawyer who was having a day she would never forget.

CHAPTER 18

Before he could face Tony Gillespie, Russell decided he needed a strong coffee.

With his cup in hand he asked Alex, "What the hell do you make of that?"

She was nursing a cup of peppermint tea in her palms, peering over the rim at her boss. "I don't know what to say. She's a lot smarter than I first thought. It looks like she has manipulated and controlled her brother for most of his life."

"Do you think he'll tell us the same story about Tim's murder?"

"I doubt that he's bright enough to lie convincingly. If he killed him we'll know."

"Should we tell him that he was Tim's father?"

"I think we should, it'll probably shake him emotionally and that should make it easier for us to get to the truth of what happened on Halloween night."

"OK, let's go see what Mr Gillespie has to say for himself."

Still clutching their drinks, the two detectives walked to the second interview room. Apart from the attending constable, Gillespie was alone. Unlike his sister he had made no attempt to smarten himself up; his stained shirt and ragged jogging trousers seemed to be an almost permanent feature.

The uniformed officer left and Russell started a new tape with the usual introductions. He asked Gillespie if he required a lawyer.

"Naw, Ah've no done anythin' wrang."

"If you change your mind at any point in this interview, please say so for the benefit of the recording."

Gillespie nodded and said, "Awright."

"How are you Mr Gillespie?" Russell asked.

"Where's ma sister?"

"She's fine. She's in the other room."

"Whit hiv you done tae her?"

"We haven't done anything to her. She's just helping us to understand what happened to Tim. She had a lot to tell us and some of it she hasn't even told you."

Gillespie was wary of a trap. "Whit kind o' stuff?"

Russell made no attempt to soften the emotional blow. "For example she told us that Tim was actually your son."

Gillespie's eyes opened wide and he shook his head. "Naw, he wis her son. No' officially but she fun' him, she raised him."

"That was a lie she told you to protect you. She gave birth to him after the two of you had sex. You're his father and she's his mother."

He continued to shake his head roughly. "Naw that's a lie. Why are ye lyin' tae me?"

Alex said softly, "It's not a lie, Mr Gillespie. We did a DNA test to confirm it."

His voice grew louder and his body language more agitated as he said, "Naw, ye're makin' it up. Ye're tryin' tae trick me."

Russell interjected firmly. "No Mr Gillespie we're not making it up. She was very willing to talk to us. In fact she told us how you killed Tim and how she helped you to try to cover it up."

Gillespie's reaction was sudden and explosive. With a wild swing of his right arm he sent Russell's mug flying from the small table, the contents splashed across the superintendent and the mug caught Alex a glancing blow on her right temple. As the drink flew across the room, Gillespie stood up and shouted, "Ye're a liar, Myra wid never say that. It's a lie, it's a lie." He started to make his way towards the detectives. Russell slammed his hand on to the strip of rubber that ran around the walls of the room, activating an alarm. A high-pitched noise filled the small space and stopped Gillespie in his tracks, before he could reach Russell and Menzies. A few seconds later the door burst open, the custody sergeant and one of the uniformed constables rushed at Gillespie and restrained him. All the time Gillespie's shouted his refrain of 'it's a lie.'

"Take him to the cells," Russell ordered. Then he said, "Mr Gillespie has had to be removed due to a violent outburst. Interview suspended at three thirty-six." As Russell's shock subsided he asked Alex, "Are you OK?"

"I…I think so."

"Look's like you might get a souvenir." Russell said pointing to the red welt that was already appearing on the side of her head. "Do you need a doctor?"

"No, I think it's just a bruise."

"Let's get out of here."

Russell guided Alex back to their office where he made her a sweet tea.

"Are you two all right?" DS Craigan asked.

"Yes, we're just a little shaken up." Russell replied.

"What was that all about?"

"I genuinely don't think he killed him," Alex said. "That reaction was not that of a guilty man."

Russell disagreed. "But it was the reaction of an angry, violent man. We've seen already that he has a short fuse; just think how he behaved when you went to pick him up. I think he's just the kind who could kill on a moment's notice, no thought, no planning just an animalistic reaction."

"I agree, sir. He's a dangerous man." Craigan said.

Alex fought her corner. "I think he only behaves like that in relation to his sister. I think he loves her completely in a way that we can't possibly understand, but unless Tim Lauchlan threatened his mother in some way, I don't see Tony being a killer."

Russell needed to be sure how to tackle Tony Gillespie when he had calmed down enough to be interviewed. He reached for his mobile phone and found Dr McNeil's contact details. He tapped on the icon to dial her number.

"Forensic pathology, Dr McNeil speaking."

"Doctor, it's Tom Russell."

"Oh hello Superintendent Russell. What can I do for you?"

"It's about the Lauchlan case. Would you be able to estimate the height of his killer?"

"Not to the centimetre, no."

"What about an approximation?"

"You know I'm not keen on guesses, Tom."

"I understand that but I need some idea. Would the killer be smaller, about the same height or considerably taller than the victim?"

She remained reluctant to commit herself. "There's nothing I can tell you that will stand up in court."

"That's fine, I'm not asking you for sworn testimony. Could the killer have been say six feet six?"

"Providing both the killer and the victim were standing on level ground, I would say the killer was around the same height as Tim Lauchlan, possibly a little shorter. The angle of penetration was almost horizontal to his shoulder blade. If the killer had been as tall as you indicate, I would have expected the wound to have been at a much steeper downward angle but don't quote me on that."

"Thanks Doc, you've been a big help."

When he had finished the call, Alex asked, "What did she say?"

"You might be right Alex. She doesn't think that the killer was taller than Lauchlan. It seems that Tony might be telling the truth."

He reached for his phone again. "Sean, it's Tom Russell. We don't need another DNA test; the woman has confirmed that your findings are correct. I need you to do something else for me. Can you get a team over to Myra and Tony Gillespie's house? Tell them I suspect that it's our primary crime scene in the murder of Tim Lauchlan. I want them to give it the works."

"Not a problem," The Irishman replied. "I'll let you know what we find." He finished the call.

"We still don't know how this relates to poor Michelle Armstrong," Alex said.

"I know, but we will. We will," he stated.

*

It was another hour before Tony Gillespie was calm enough to be interviewed. He was handcuffed as he sat disconsolately across from the two detectives, a uniformed constable standing watch over him. He was asked once more if he needed a lawyer and once more he turned down the offer.

"Mr Gillespie, would you like to tell us your version of events on Halloween?"

After a slight pause, he related much the same story as his sister had told but with one major difference, she was the one who wielded the screwdriver.

"Why was your sister so angry?" Russell asked when the larger man had finished his tale.

"She tellt him that he wis an ungrateful bastard. That she hud gi'en up a lot for him. That we needed the money he brought in, but he jist laughed at her and said that she'd need to go oot and work rather than sponge aff o' him. That wis when she went mental. She slapped him and he laughed again. He turned away and went to walk oot the door tae ma room. She reached intae the drawer, pulled oot the screwdriver, went tae ma bedroom and stabbed him in the neck. She was so angry Ah couldnae stoap her. She made me wrap him in the rug and then tellt me tae get a van. Ah dae some casual work drivin' fur a wee courier in Maryhill Road. Ah goat a van fae him - she tellt me tae tell him that Ah wis helpin' a pal tae move hoose. Ah hud tae take Tim's boady doon tae the van. She tellt me Ah hud tae wait till late at night before takin' him tae the cemetery. She knew where that guy wis buried as ma mother hud shown her his grave. Ma maw wis fascinated by murder, so she wis."

"What did you think about Tim wanting to leave?"

"Ah wis pleased, if he went away it wid be jist me an Myra. That's whit Ah always wanted."

"Why did she want you to leave Tim's body in the cemetery?"

"She thought that you'd think it wis the same as that wummin that wis found oan the grave in the Necropolis. She said youse widnae think we hud anythin' tae dae wi' his death."

"How did you get into the cemetery?"

"Cut the padlock and drove the van tae where she tellt me tae go."

"Thanks for your co-operation Mr Gillespie. Can I ask you why did you decide to help us?"

"When Ah wis sittin' in that cell, Ah realised that she disnae love me any mair. She wis jist trying tae get me tae take the blame fur whit she hud done."

The interview over, Gillespie was led away. Russell was positive that although he was an accessory to the crime, Gillespie wasn't the one who had committed the murder. He would have to speak to the Fiscal to find out what charges she wanted to bring against Tony Gillespie but it was not a priority, it could wait until the reports had been filed.

The next task was to complete the formalities and charge Myra Gillespie with her son's murder. She sat completely still and stared at Russell as he read the charge. Once again she appeared divorced from proceedings as if she were watching a TV drama. When he asked her if she had anything to say, she simply shook her head. She was led away by a female constable.

Russell still had to speak to the Fiscal and the ACC to let them know of the developments but he told the team that they should finish up for the night. There would be plenty of time to complete the detailed reports the following day. Alex for one, was glad to escape the station, the day had left her feeling dirty somehow.

*

She arrived back at her flat at five thirty and spent the next thirty minutes under a hot, pounding shower. She scrubbed herself clean of the memories of the devious, sociopathic killer and the Gillespies' creepy incestuous relationship. Myra Gillespie was one of the strangest women she had ever met. There appeared to be no real maternal bond to her son - Alex thought that maybe the nature of his conception had put a barrier between them before he was even born, or maybe she had no emotional connection to anyone and that her brother had filled a purely physical need.

When she felt clean again she ate some noodles and chicken cooked in a packet sauce. The meal over, she decided that she had to speak to Noel. She hadn't heard from him since they had met on the day Tim Lauchlan's body had been found.

She felt a nervous flutter in her stomach as she drove to his home. She was hoping he was going to be there as she hadn't called ahead, worried that she wouldn't be able to go through with it if she heard a tone in his voice that indicated he was ready to leave her behind.

When he opened the door, his handsome face was set in a stern mien. She walked through the hall and glanced into his bedroom where she could see a pile of boxes, some already sealed with tape, others lying open waiting for contents.

"So you're going then?"

"Yes, Alex. I'm going. I've handed in my notice and I'll be away by the end of the month." There was sadness in his attitude but also a feeling that his mind was made up and nothing she could say now would make the slightest difference. As they walked into his living room, he put as much physical distance between the two of them as possible, as if he wanted to emphasise the emotional expanse that existed in their relationship.

"I don't want you to go," she said faintly.

"Not enough though, eh Alex?"

"I'm sorry, I don't know what's wrong with me."

"You'll need to work that out on your own. I can't put my life on hold for you any longer."

"I know and I don't want you to but I'm not in a place where I can make the kind of commitment that you want."

"I understand that and it makes me sad but I need this new job in a new town for my own sake. If you can't move our relationship on, then I need the change that this job will give me. I want a new challenge that doesn't include dead bodies and pointing my camera at people on the worst day of their lives. I can't do that every day if I can't come home to a relationship that is solid and based on trust."

"I know. I know. I'm so sorry." She started to cry but he made no move to comfort her. At that point she knew that it was indeed over and that she had driven away a man who had been nothing but good for her. She left the flat dabbing away tears with a paper hanky, there was nothing left to do.

*

Russell went to Wishaw to visit his brother. Eddie was feeling better and the doctor was pleased with his progress. The brothers suffered an awkward conversation that simply emphasised the gap between them. Even as children they had been very different people but now that difference was even more pronounced. Russell was glad when the visiting bell rang and he could go home. On his journey home his only thought was as bad as things were with Eddie at least the two of them weren't members of the Gillespie family.

CHAPTER 19

The first thing Alex did the following morning was to call Tom Russell and ask him if she could have the day off. He knew that there was something wrong with her but she didn't give him any details, and he decided she would tell him if and when she was ready. As the Lauchlan case only required final reports to be written and evidence checked, he agreed to her taking some time.

He spent the morning at Maryhill station, supervising the team as they completed the case. Many of the detectives had already returned to their regular duties in their home stations and by the end of the day the information on the incident board would be filed away, the remaining officers would be back investigating muggings; theft and assaults, and the Lauchlan murder case would be in the hands of the Fiscal.

The forensic team had gone through the Gillespie house looking for links to both murders. Nothing they found indicated that Lauchlan was involved in any way with Michelle Armstrong's murder. Although it was what he had expected,

Russell had hoped that Sean and his team would find the poison or something that would have linked the two cases.

When Russell called him, ACC Baxter had expressed his congratulations to the team but also his disappointment that the Michelle Armstrong murder remained an open case. Russell's patience with his commanding officer was never very long but he was sanguine about the criticism as he was equally frustrated by the failure to wrap up the young woman's murder.

After a brief lunch at a nearby fast-food restaurant, Russell drove to Helen Street and his own office. He was sitting staring at the Michelle Armstrong incident board when Ann-Marie Craigan walked in.

"Hoping for inspiration, sir?"

"Aye, you could say that. I know we've missed something but I have no idea what that something is."

"Is Lauchlan the key?"

"I think Tim Lauchlan knew who killed Michelle. Let's presume he was blackmailing the killer, but how did he know who the killer was?"

The two detectives gazed at the board for nearly ten minutes before Ann-Marie Craigan said, "What if the killer had researched the Sarah Maitland killing in the library?"

Russell pulled himself up from the slouched position he had adopted. "Go on."

"If he knew the killer - maybe it was someone he had met in the Cuppa Joe café. That person visited the library and asked to see the same newspapers you were looking for. When you went to the library to find out more about Sarah

Maitland's murder, he put two and two together and started blackmailing Michelle Armstrong's killer."

He was interested in what she was saying but there was something nagging at him. "What motive would a customer have to kill Michelle Armstrong?"

Ann-Marie's enthusiasm dispersed and she sighed. "I have no idea."

"Let's go back to basics. We know there are three main motives for murder - money, revenge and love, passion, lust, whatever you want to call it."

"Agreed."

"Did we check out Michelle's will? Who benefitted financially?"

Ann-Marie turned to a computer and logged in. She sifted the database for the information. "Her parents kept half of her estate and the rest went to Janet Kerry including Michelle's half of the business."

"We can definitely rule out the parents. Janet Kerry had an alibi?"

A few more key presses and the answer appeared on the screen. "Yes, she was at the cinema with another friend. Both the other woman and a member of staff confirmed that she was there until ten thirty."

"Could she have still killed Michelle?"

"Possibly but why would she be the one to report Michelle as missing?"

"Stranger things have happened, in this case alone." Russell smiled weakly but there was no doubt that Janet Kerry made for an unlikely killer. "If we rule out money, what about revenge?"

"We ruled out Kyle Allen's family and friends, and nothing pointed to Michelle having made enemies through something else she did."

"So that leaves love."

"We ruled out Michelle's ex-lovers but maybe we got it wrong. What if it had something to do with Nick Jackson?"

"A jealous ex-lover sees him out with another woman, that kind if thing."

"Exactly."

Russell played devil's advocate once more. "And she just so happened to have strychnine and a wedding dress to hand?"

"Maybe she stalked him. Determined to make sure that if she couldn't have him, no one could, so she made preparations in advance." It sounded a bit unlikely to Craigan as she said it but she was sure that it was a possibility that Nick Jackson was the root of the jealousy.

"It's conceivable but as a theory it's a bit all over the place."

Not to be dissuaded she pressed on. "Jackson said that Michelle was the first woman he had met through the dating site that he felt a real connection with. Judging by what he said, he had been using the site for sometime. What if we get the details of the women on the list and find out if any of the names jump out at us?"

"Did we get a warrant?"

"No, DI Menzies got Jackson's address before we were able to organise one."

"Let's do that. You never know it might just start to join the dots. Can you get that arranged?"

"Of course."

Craigan went back to her own desk and began the process of getting the warrant to look at the website's records. Russell could hear her arguing her case as she was questioned about whether she had probable cause to ask for the information. She impressed him with her debating skills and confidence in her argument.

He heard her say, "That's great thank you." When she had finished she shouted to him, "Got it, sir. Will I get the Stirling guys to serve it?"

"No, it's OK. I'll go."

He was simply relieved to move the Armstrong case out of neutral and start it going forward once more.

He picked up the warrant and drove to Stirling. The website's owner was extremely uncomfortable that his data was being taken out of his control, but he complied with the official document and handed Russell a data stick containing a spreadsheet listing all of his client details. The database was designed to prevent anyone knowing who had met with whom. Russell was disappointed but thanked the man for his help.

He was back in the office by five but decided that one more day in the hunt for Michelle Armstrong's killer wouldn't make much difference. Whoever the killer might be was either out of the country or feeling comfortable that they had got away with it.

*

Alex had gone back to her bed after she had spoken to Russell that morning. When she finally roused herself around noon she knew there was only one place to go.

Her drive to Ayrshire to see her parents was completed in a violent storm of wind and rain over the Fenwick Moor. With windscreen wipers working at full capacity it took her longer than usual to make the journey.

Her father was waiting with an open door when she pulled up in front of their house.

"Whit's up?" he asked as she walked up the short path. Tears flowed again and once again her dad was there to pick up the pieces of her love life.

When she had finished the story of Noel and his decision to move south, she could tell that her father was disappointed while her mother's face gave nothing away. When she and Noel had first started to go out she had worried about what her father's reaction to him would be. There aren't too many black faces in Ayrshire, and her father was an old-fashioned kind of man who she thought might not approve of her daughter's choice of partner. She felt ashamed that she had so misjudged him; the man who had raised her took an immediate and unconditional shine to Noel. On their first visit together, Noel disappeared with her dad off to the pub while she got a chance to tell her mother how she felt about the big Londoner. When her Dad and Noel arrived back having had a drink or two they were laughing and debating the merits of various football players. On subsequent visits her father and Noel had become firm friends and it was now clear that her dad felt she had made the wrong choice in letting a man she loved go.

"He's no' Andrew, but it's your choice, pet," was all her father said. He left Alex with her mother in the kitchen and went to tinker with something in his garage.

"He's right, isn't he?" she asked her mum.

"He is. Noel's a different character from Andrew but you have to do what's right for you."

Her mother and father's reaction only helped to make her feel worse. She knew they were correct but even if she changed her mind about living with Noel, it was too late. She felt a sense of relief when a text arrived from Russell.

Need you back tomorrow. We might have a break in the Armstrong case.

At least she knew what her immediate future held, even if beyond that was unclear.

CHAPTER 20

The following day rain and gale force winds - the remnants of an Atlantic storm - battered Alex on her journey to Helen Street. The conditions were so bad that the rain was finding it's way through the seal of the car's windscreen causing a little puddle to form on the top of the dashboard.

I really need a new car, she thought for the hundredth time.

When she had found a parking space in the station car park, she placed a tissue on the puddle and left it there to collect any further leaks.

Before she went to her desk she looked in to Russell's office. As usual he was there, the first to work every day.

"Good morning, sir."

He looked up from his one-fingered typing. "Hello Alex. Did you have a good day off?"

"Not really."

"Do you want to talk about it?" he said gesturing at the chair on the opposite side of the desk.

She sat down, gulped away the temptation to cry and said, "It's over between Noel and I. He's resigned and is going to Manchester to work."

"I'm sorry to hear that, Alex. I like Noel and he's a bloody good crime-scene photographer. What happened between you?"

"I couldn't give him what he wanted. I couldn't bring myself to trust him enough to share my life with him and he says that he needed something in his life to change, and if I wasn't going to offer that change he had to find it through his work."

"My relationship with Karen was strained by her unreasonable jealousy, to the point that it drove me from her. I can understand Noel's reaction but I also understand that you were hurt by Andrew."

She sighed. "A part of me thinks I should be over that by now but I just don't want that to happen again."

"I'm sure there are plenty that would say the same to me. I should be over Karen as she was my ex-wife, it's all in the past, but emotions are never that simple."

Reluctant to analyse further what had happened, Alex said, "What's this about a break in the case?"

"DS Craigan and I had a little brainstorming session yesterday. We talked through possible motives and the one we hadn't really looked at in any detail was Nick Jackson."

"I thought we had agreed that he wasn't capable of it."

"No, not him directly. Remember what Kyle Allen's mate said about his girlfriend?"

"That she was a bit of a bunny boiler."

"What if one of Nick Jackson's ex-girlfriends was so obsessed with him that she was willing to kill anyone who went out with him."

"I don't know, sir, it sounds a bit of a stretch for someone to plan this crime on the basis of a single date."

"Ann-Marie and I thought that the killer could have basically planned the murder for anyone and Michelle Armstrong was the unfortunate one that tipped this woman over the edge."

Alex was still sceptical but said, "How do you plan to find this woman?"

"I got a warrant for the client information from the dating site. Jackson said that he had a number of connections through the site. We thought it would be a good place to start."

Despite her pain, she was pleased to see Russell so enthused and engaged again. Maybe his personal healing was progressing.

"I'll grab a tea and get started."

"It might take a while, there are five thousand four hundred women subscribed to the site."

"Oh joy."

Ann-Marie Craigan had arrived by the time Alex walked into the main office. She was sitting at her desk, the printer behind her was spitting out sheet after sheet of paper.

"Are you OK?" the Irish woman asked.

"I'll tell you later," Alex replied with a dejected look.

"Have you spoken to the boss?"

"Yes, he told me about the warrant."

"I'm just printing off the details now. I thought it might be easier to go through it in printed form than stare at computer screens."

"The stationery budget will take a hit." Alex replied with a grin.

"I won't tell him if you don't." The two women laughed. "I've narrowed the list down to those that live in Glasgow and the West Of Scotland. There's still three thousand names but it's a start."

"Do you think we'll find something?"

"It's better than nothing I suppose."

Tea by her side, Alex sat at her desk with one half of the pile of printouts. She picked up a highlighter and began the boring task of reading through the long list of names. An hour passed and the only thing she had found is just how much she hated clerical jobs.

"Oh my god," Ann-Marie Craigan exclaimed.

"What? Have you found someone?"

"Yes, but unfortunately she's probably not our killer. Come and have a look at this."

Alex moved to join the DS. On the desk was a profile of one Jacqui Kerr. As she read the details, she realised that it was indeed the Procurator Fiscal. She laughed heartily and her humour infected Craigan who shared in her mirth.

"What's the big joke?" Russell said as he joined them.

"It seems our noted Fiscal is looking for love," Alex managed through the giggles.

"Ladies that isn't a very professional attitude," Russell replied.

"I know but I can't help it," Alex replied and laughed once more.

Russell couldn't hold out any longer and began to laugh as hard as the two women. The hilarity was so infectious that some of the other teams were soon chuckling with no real clue as to what they were laughing about.

It took five minutes for a semblance of normality to return by which time every cop in the station knew about the Fiscal's love search. Russell left them to it and tried to ensure that it wouldn't go any further than the office but somehow he knew that this piece of juicy gossip would be spread around every station in the city before the day was out.

After another hour of ploughing through the records with no success Alex said, "Can't we just interview Jackson again?"

"The boss was a bit wary of doing that. Jackson didn't react very well the last time we spoke to him."

"That was in the station and he was a suspect. If we go to him as a witness he might be able to help."

"Anything's better than sitting here ticking off names."

Alex went to Russell with her suggestion. She got the impression that his reluctance came more from a sense of embarrassment at his own behaviour when he had interviewed Jackson rather than the man's reaction to it. After some cajoling, he eventually agreed.

*

Nick Jackson's web-design company was based in a block of offices in the Finnieston district of the city. The office overlooked the saucer shape of the new concert venue and the less attractive site of the shed that was known as the Scottish Exhibition and Conference Centre. There were around a dozen desks, each with at least one huge monitor. In one corner there was a ping-pong table, a pool table and a variety of food and drink. The members of staff were dressed casually and there was a relaxed atmosphere.

Russell and Menzies were guided to Jackson's office, a glass-sided room at the corner of the floor.

'Nick, these police officers want to speak to you."

An immediate look of dread haunted his face.

Russell moved to calm him. "Mr Jackson, you're not a suspect, we're simply here for some help."

It seemed to have the desired effect as the tension left Jackson's face. "I'm not sure how I can help."

"Mr Jackson we are looking at the possibility that Michelle Armstrong's killer was known to you."

"What?"

"We're working on the theory that the killer is a woman, one who you may have dated at one time."

"You're kidding. You think she was killed because I took her on a date?"

"It's one theory we're working on." Russell felt that letting him know that it was the only theory they had was not a good idea.

"I can't believe this. Who would do that?"

"That's what we're hoping you would be able to help us with."

He shrugged his shoulders. "I wouldn't know where to start."

"Let's start with anyone you dated through caledonialove. com."

"Give me a moment." He pulled his computer keyboard towards him and began tapping rapidly. A few clicks of the mouse and the printer on the cabinets to his left sprang to life. "These are the five women that I was matched with and went out with."

Russell took the list and scanned it, one name jumped out. "Jacqui Kerr, when did you go out with her?"

"No, it couldn't be her. We only went out last night. It wasn't a roaring success, I don't think I'll be seeing her again."

"Alex…"

"I know, ring the Fiscal." She stepped out of the office.

There were no names on the list that were related to the case but Russell asked, "Is there one of these women whose behaviour you thought was strange?"

"They were all interested in what I did and how much I earned, except this one."

He pointed to the fourth name on the list, Ruth Nixon. "We went out three times and all she wanted to do was talk about me. She didn't want to tell me anything about herself, she asked about my parents; my siblings; what school I went to; who else I had gone out with; it was endless. On the third date I gave her an ultimatum that if she wouldn't tell me more, I would end it. She said that there was nothing interesting about her and begged me to go out with her. It was only later I realised that she had changed her Facebook status to 'in a relationship' with me, and that she had left it like that even after I had told her I didn't want to see her again. I tried to tell her to change it but she refused. In the end I deleted her as a friend."

"Can I see a picture?"

Jackson typed on the keyboard and then swung his screen around so Russell could see it.

"Shit, I know that woman. That's not Ruth Nixon, that's Patricia Lockhart, she was one of Michelle's customers."

At that moment Alex opened the door and said, "I can't get a hold of the Fiscal and no one has seen her all day."

CHAPTER 21

Russell sprang from his chair. "Shit. She might be in trouble. Do you know where Nixon lives?" he asked Jackson.

"It says Glasgow on her profile but I'm not sure if that's true. As I said earlier, she wasn't very forthcoming about her life. Could Jacqui really be in trouble?"

"Let's hope not. Thanks for your help." The two detectives rushed from the office. Russell reached for his phone. "Ann-Marie, take a uniformed bod and get to the Procurator Fiscal's house. Her office will give you the address."

"Why? What's up?"

"I'll explain later but it's important that we find her."

"She's missing?"

"She didn't call in today, she's not answering her phone and she was out on a date with Nick Jackson last night."

"Oh crap."

"Exactly. Get a call out to every car and station; let them know to look out for her. Call me with any information."

"Yes, sir. Where will you be?"

"DI Menzies and I will be looking for a woman called Patricia Lockhart. She might be our killer."

As the call had progressed they reached his car. He hung up and the tyres screeched as he pulled away before the traction control kicked in. He lit up the blue lights and blared the siren. Memories of another race flooded through his mind and threatened to overwhelm him.

"Are you OK? Do you want me to drive?" Alex said as he wove erratically through the traffic.

"I'm fine," he snapped.

It was a short journey to the Cuppa Joe café. Russell slammed on the brakes right outside the door, double-parked; the car was blocking the narrow street.

He burst in the door and caused the patrons to stare in amazement. Janet Kerry stepped out from behind the counter. "What's wrong?"

"Patricia Lockhart. Where does she work?"

"Eh…"

"Hurry up woman, this is important."

"It's Davies and Nolan, the chartered surveyors. It's in the first crescent off Sauchiehall Street. What's this all about?"

"I can't explain now," he shouted as he walked away.

When he was back in the car, he reversed back from the café towards the entrance to the street drawing an irritated beep from the car behind him. He ignored the sound, jerked the steering to his right and turned towards the crescent of Victorian former townhouses that were home to a number of businesses and ran parallel to Sauchiehall Street.

"We're looking for Davies and Nolan," he told Alex.

They were nearly at the end of the crescent when Alex shouted, "There."

The cars brakes got another workout and Russell was out once again abandoning the car rather than park it.

The chartered surveyors' office occupied the whole building. Russell was buzzed into an airy reception area.

A middle-aged woman in a navy blue business suit greeted him. "Can I help you?"

Brandishing his warrant card Russell said, "Detective Superintendent Tom Russell. I need to find the address of one of your employees. It's a matter of urgency."

"I'm afraid we don't give out that kind of information without good cause."

"How about perverting the course of justice and being a possible accessory to murder? Does that constitute good cause?" he barked.

The woman became flustered. "Who… what address do you need?"

"Patricia Lockhart."

"Patricia? She didn't come in today. Is she in danger?"

"No, she is the danger. Now get me the bloody address!"

The woman spent a short time consulting her computer before she gave him an address in Bridge Of Allan, a good hour away when driving within the speed limit.

"Thank you for your co-operation," Russell said as he departed.

Back in the car he hammered his foot down on the accelerator. "She's in fuckin' Bridge Of Allan. Ring Stirling and tell them to get a car to this address." He handed Alex the paper the woman had given him. "Tell them that they've to take a watching brief only. I don't want them barging in there with their size twelve boots."

She did as he asked, emphasising the need for the uniformed officers to keep their distance.

The lights and sirens got them to the M8 within a couple of minutes. Russell drove as fast as the road conditions and traffic would allow. Shouting occasionally at any driver who was slow to react to the warning sound of the siren.

"What the hell was Kerr doing going on a fuckin' date with someone we had interviewed?"

"We had ruled him out as a suspect and we had no idea that he might be the motive. Maybe she already had him on her match list and thought why not."

Russell swore under his breath.

The rain began to fall more heavily, the wind throwing it horizontally at the windscreen, causing Russell to turn the wipers up to full speed but even then visibility wasn't great. He left the M8 at the M80 exit where the traffic was a little lighter and he felt that he could push the speed up a bit. He drove in autopilot while his mind drifted to another motorway and another frantic dash to save a life. Could it really all be happening again?

His phone rang. "Get that will you?"

"It's Ann-Marie." Alex picked up the phone from the centre console of the car. "Ann-Marie, any news?"

"No sign of Ms Kerr. Her car's here but the house is locked up."

"OK thanks. We're on our way to Bridge Of Allan. Can you liaise with the Stirling team? Make sure no one goes near Patricia Lockhart's house."

"Understood."

When the call was over, Alex relayed the information to Russell.

"Shit. I hope we're not too late."

The engine revs climbed as he pressed the accelerator a little harder. The rain was still falling although it had eased from the torrent that had come down as they left Glasgow.

Half an hour later the car pulled into the street where Patricia Lockhart lived. It was comprised of a combination of substantial Victorian villas and large Edwardian family homes.

Russell drew alongside a marked police car and rolled down his window.

"Where is she?"

The constable who was in the driver's seat said, "The Lockhart house is three down on the left, sir."

"Any movement?"

"Nothing in or out."

"Do you have a battering ram?"

"Yes, sir."

"Follow me."

Russell steered his car up the drive to the front door of a stunning Edwardian house. It was painted pale blue and sat in spacious grounds. Russell sprung from his seat without even switching off the engine.

Alex did turn the key in the ignition before she joined him.

"Police," he shouted at the door as he pressed and held the doorbell. When the two constables had retrieved the battering ram from the boot of their car Russell ordered, "Open it."

It took only one swing to burst the lock. Russell was first through the gap and shouted, "Alex, I'll check upstairs." He bounded up the steps two at a time and ran from room to room but there was no one there.

Back downstairs the constables in conjunction with Alex had also found nothing.

'There's a summerhouse out back," Alex said.

"Let's have a look." Russell reached for the kitchen door and was surprised to see that it was unlocked. The two detectives ran across the lawn to the building that was reminiscent of a log cabin. There was a padlock on the door. Russell looked around to find something to break it. He picked up a stone from a rockery and hammered the lock. It took three attempts to smash the mechanism. The door swung open on to the sight of Jacqui Kerr lying naked on an old, stained mattress.

"Oh no." Russell stopped. The memories of that night eighteen months previously paralysed him. He just couldn't bring himself to reach out and touch the cold skin of another dead woman.

Alex took control and bent to feel Jacqui Kerr's pulse. "She's alive," she said with relief.

'What's that noise?" Russell said.

"Garage doors."

"Fuck. You get an ambulance," he shouted to Alex as he ran back towards the house. He charged through the house in time to see a blue Jaguar XE speed through the gates and out on to the street.

He ran to his car. He couldn't reverse as the marked car was sitting directly behind him, so he spun the wheel of the car and drove through flowerbeds and across the front lawn, and began the pursuit. The uniformed constable hadn't needed to be told to follow him.

Once on to the street Russell hammered the accelerator pedal again, simultaneously flicking the switch for the lights and sirens.

Lockhart's car was already about four hundred yards in front of him. Russell hoped that he would be able to keep up with her when they reached the motorway. She was driving north towards a roundabout that would take her on to the M9. She swung on to the roundabout and then off at the first exit, which meant she was heading south towards Glasgow. The traffic on the roundabout stopped to allow Russell to follow her.

Once he was safely on the motorway he reached for his Airwave radio. "This is Detective Superintendent Tom Russell."

"This is Control,"

"I'm in pursuit of a suspect driving a navy blue Jaguar XE going south on the M9. I have one marked car with me but we need support if we're going to box her in."

"Understood. I'll despatch two further cars from Stirling."

"Get the helicopter in the air as well."

"Sorry, sir, we can't due to the weather."

"Damn it. OK, Russell out."

He left the unit switched on so he could hear how the operation was being co-ordinated.

Lockhart drove confidently and despite Russell's speedometer showing that he was travelling at over ninety miles per hour, he was making no progress in reducing her lead.

As the chase continued, he heard over the radio that a further two cars were being despatched from Cumbernauld. Lockhart sped south towards Glasgow and joined the M80 from the M9, weaving between the other vehicles on the road. At the Castlecary Arches, the traffic was heavier and the radio announced that two marked cars were ahead of the suspect, waiting to box her in.

"Yes, got her," he said.

The rain was once again falling like a tropical storm, whipped along by the strong wind. He could see the blue lights up ahead and so did Patricia Lockhart. Realising that she was about to be trapped, she tried to brake hard to take the Cumbernauld turn off. The amount of water on the tarmac meant the Jaguar lost traction and the back end spun round. It turned through three hundred and sixty degrees as it careered across two lanes of the slip road. By a miracle it avoided any other vehicle before it crashed sideways in to a small copse of trees.

Russell gasped in horror as he watched the accident unfold. He slowed and turned down the slip road where he stopped opposite the battered car. He ran down a slope and opened the car door. Deflating airbags surrounded Lockhart and although bruised, she appeared to have been lucky. He loosened her seatbelt and helped her from the car. She was dazed but it didn't stop him putting her in cuffs, reading her rights to her and informing her of the charges against her.

*

Back in the summerhouse Alex discovered that Jacqui Kerr had been sedated and was sleeping peacefully, so Alex left her for a short time to get some clothes. The ambulance arrived twenty minutes after the call. The paramedics confirmed that all vital signs were fine and that she would simply need time to shake off the effects of whatever drug had been used on her. Alex sat in the ambulance as they drove to Forth Valley hospital. When the doctors were satisfied that the paramedics diagnosis was correct, they sent the Fiscal to a ward. Alex was given permission to sit with her until she woke up.

It was half an hour before Jacqui Kerr began to recover. She opened her eyes, noticed Alex and said groggily, "DI Menzies?"

"Yes."

"Where… where am I?"

Alex stood up and poured a glass of water from the bedside cabinet as she said, "You're in Forth Valley hospital. Here have a drink."

Kerr took the glass and sipped from it. "What happened?"

"You don't remember?"

"No."

Alex told her about Patricia Lockhart and the theory that she had killed Michelle Armstrong. When she mentioned Nick Jackson a glint of recognition appeared.

"We had a date," Kerr said.

"That's right."

"I don't remember what happened," her eyes began to close once more.

"You get some rest. Maybe it'll come back to you."

Alex left her in the care of the nurses, with a policeman posted outside the door to her room.

CHAPTER 22

Lockhart was taken to the Royal Infirmary in Glasgow for a thorough medical check before she could be taken to the station for interview. Although there were no serious injuries the doctors decided to keep her in for observation, so it was the following day before the detectives had a chance to talk to her.

The interview was conducted in Helen Street station with her lawyer in attendance.

Russell had surprised Alex by asking her to take the lead, so it was she that did the introductions.

The biggest problem the detectives faced was the lack of physical evidence linking her to Michelle Armstrong's murder. A search of her house had failed to find neither Michelle's DNA nor any trace of strychnine. It meant that the questions were restricted to the kidnapping of Jacqui Kerr - who had no memory of what had happened after she left Nick Jackson.

"Ms Lockhart would you like to explain why you abducted Procurator Fiscal Kerr."

Lockhart's haughty attitude was still in evidence as she replied, "I was protecting a friend."

"Protecting a friend? Would that friend's name be Nick Jackson by any chance?"

"That's not for me to say."

"If not you, who?"

"That's between me and my friend. I don't need to tell you anything."

"You're absolutely correct, but let's go on the premise that this 'friend' is Nick Jackson. He has told us that he wants nothing to do with you. That he doesn't even like you, never mind regard you as a friend."

"He wants to keep what we have private, he's a very discreet person."

Alex had at least got Lockhart to admit that Nick Jackson was the source of her jealousy. She pressed her advantage by exaggerating Jackson's feelings. "No, he can't stand you. In fact he told us that if he never sees you again it'll be too soon."

"Of course he wouldn't tell you that he loves me," Lockhart replied dismissively.

"If he loves you, why is he going out with other women? Women like Jacqui Kerr or Michelle Armstrong for instance."

Lockhart's lawyer, who was a weaselly little man with over-sized glasses and horrible grey suit, decided to interrupt, "My client is only here to answer questions with regards to Ms Kerr."

Russell broke his silence. "I'm sure your client knows exactly why she's here." It was delivered in a warning tone that was all too familiar to Alex. Lawyers were not his favourite people.

Lockhart remained aloof, as if the process demeaned her in some way.

Alex tried again. "If Mr Jackson has such strong feelings for you, why is he registered on a dating site? Why is he going out on dates with other women?"

"They're trying to trick him. They'll harm him if I don't protect him."

"Exactly how are you protecting him?"

Suddenly Lockhart's face changed and contorted into a snarl. "I won't let any of them hurt him like the last time."

"The last time? Who hurt him before?"

"Jessica bloody Turner."

"Who is Jessica Turner?"

"You should know. You should know who she is."

Russell put his hand on Alex's arm. "Suspend the interview."

Alex did as he requested and they left the room together.

"What's up?" she asked.

"If she thinks we should know about Jessica Turner, there must be a reason. Let's see if records can give us anything."

They went to Alex desk where she searched the records for Jessica Turner. She found a record dating from 2012 about a fatal accident on the M9. Jessica Turner had died in a car driven by David Kinniburgh. The report was completely factual with nothing to connect the incident to Lockhart. Alex turned to her web search engine once more and that produced the results they needed.

A newspaper story from two days after the accident reported the salacious details.

GROOM DIES AFTER A NIGHT OF PASSION WITH BRIDESMAID.

David Kinniburgh, who was killed in a car accident on Tuesday night, was having an affair with his future bride's best friend.

Mr Kinniburgh and Ms Jessica Turner were returning to Bridge of Allan after a passionate night at the Hilton Hotel. Mr Kinniburgh was due to marry Ms Patricia Lockhart at Dunblane Cathedral this Saturday but friends of Ms Turner say she and the groom had been having an affair for some time.

There were pictures of all three who had been caught in the tragic triangle.

"Who does he look like?" Russell said.

There was no doubt the Nick Jackson bore an uncanny resemblance to David Kinniburgh.

Back in the room, Alex continued the interview.

"Tell us about Jessica's affair with David."

Lockhart's snarl returned. "That whore, she killed him. She killed Nick."

"Patricia, Nick is very much alive and well."

Lockhart looked confused momentarily before she said, "David, I meant David."

"So why would you need to protect Nick?"

"David, I need to protect David."

"But David's dead,"

Her confusion deepened. "No, no he's not. I had to protect him from that bitch Michelle. She was going to steal him from me and kill him."

"So you had to protect him from Michelle?"

The lawyer moved to interrupt but Russell cut him off, "Let her speak if she wants to."

Alex repeated the question.

Lockhart who was muddled replied defiantly, "She was boasting in that café how she was going on a date with David. She told me they were going to that fancy club of his. I watched her go in with him and then they came out and she kissed him. That was it; I knew what she had planned. She was going to lure him in and lead him to his death, just like the last time. I called her mobile and told her I was working late at the office and thought I saw someone trying to break in to the café. I told her I would meet her there. I drove to the café and she arrived in a taxi about fifteen minutes later. I helped her look around the building and she said that everything was fine. I invited her back to the office for a coffee, told her I would drive her home afterwards. I made the coffee and slipped the poison into it. The silly woman had no idea what was happening as she began to struggle to breathe. I told her that she was not going to harm my David. I watched her gasp for breath and then she vomited everywhere. I had to clean it up." The final sentence was said as if it was the most disgusting thing that had happened that night. Even the lawyer looked a little shocked.

"Where did Michelle die?"

"In the basement of my company's building. I knew what was going to happen to her, so I took her down to the basement. Once the poison took effect it was a mess. She was filthy, so I undressed her, and washed her down with a bucket of water. Then I put her in my great-grandmother's wedding dress and believe me it wasn't easy. It was the dress I was supposed to wear before she took David from me."

The two men and the two tragic incidents were entirely meshed together in her mind.

Alex prompted the end of the story. "Then you took her to the Necropolis."

Her tone changed and she seemed almost wistful. "I took her there just after dawn. She looked so pretty. Just like I had imagined I would have looked in that dress."

"Did Tim Lauchlan know what you had done?"

"Who?"

"The man from the library."

She switched again, back to her angry persona. "Oh that vile little toad. When I was researching how to protect David, I asked him for the newspapers about the Sarah Maitland murder. I remembered that story, how her best friend had betrayed her. I wanted to recreate it, so I could get revenge for poor Sarah as well as to protect my David. The librarian worked out what I had done and he had the temerity to blackmail me. I didn't want to but I had to pay up to protect David."

Alex suspended the interview once again. There was no more to learn, although the lawyer would have a field day with the confusion the woman was suffering. A psychiatric evaluation was now going to be necessary.

Back in the office, Russell was simply relieved it was over. The psychiatrists and lawyers could argue the toss all they wanted, the MIT had done their job.

*

Jacqui Kerr's abduction proved to be a similar story. Lockhart had taken to stalking Jackson and when she saw him with the Fiscal, she followed her after the date. Kerr had gone to drown her sorrows with a drink as the meeting had been a disaster. Lockhart started speaking to her and slipped Rohypnol into a glass of red wine.

Kerr remembered nothing after her time with Jackson. Tom Russell had taken Kerr's statement himself.

"Why did you go out with him?" he asked when the formalities were concluded.

She looked abashed. "I'm lonely, Superintendent. You don't know how difficult it is to isolate oneself from other people when you are their managerial superior. My work doesn't allow much time for socialising outside of the office, and I have to keep my distance from those I work with. I joined the dating site as a way of breaking that cycle. I recognised his name when it came up on my match list, and I believed that maybe fate had intervened, so I decided to meet him."

It was difficult for Russell to understand Kerr's position. Russell couldn't grasp the woman's need to be aloof from those around her. He always believed you had to treat your colleagues with respect and be a willing ear for them. You had to relate to each other on a human level or the team would struggle to function. It gave him an insight to Kerr's icy demeanour, and an understanding of how she had used it as a form of defence mechanism. Her choice to connect with Nick Jackson was so out of character he said, "You don't seem like the kind of person who would make decisions based on fate."

"I don't but..." She let the sentence hang, heavy with a vulnerability that Russell would never have suspected her capable of.

He felt her desperation and the loneliness that had seen her reach for anything to alleviate it. "That decision nearly cost you dearly."

"I know but thanks to you it didn't. Don't worry I won't be making any more radical life choices based on kismet, feelings or fate." She surprised him by planting an uncharacteristic kiss on his cheek. "Thank you, Detective Superintendent."

It was a shame that her experience was likely to drive her even further into the protective shell of caustic sarcasm and barbed comments that she had used as long as he had known her. Any hope that she might lead a happier, more fulfilled life seemed to have gone.

For his part he realised that it was time for him to join humanity again and build a better life.

EPILOGUE

Once again he found himself at the doors of Mairead's church. The case was four weeks in the past and more mundane work had taken its place. He wasn't sure why he had come but something in him wanted to tell the friendly cleric about what had happened to him.

He sat in the pews once more until she arrived.

"If it isn't my favourite non-believer," she said with a welcoming smile.

"I hope you don't mind me popping in."

"Not at all. What can I do for you?"

"I needed a neutral ear."

"Which one would you prefer?" she said indicating each of her ears in turn.

"The last eighteen months have been pretty hellish but I think I might be ready to move on. Is eighteen months too short a time to grieve?"

"Tom, I've known people who are still grieving after twenty years while others who are ready to move on within six months. There is no definitive time; there is no definitive way to move on. Your heart will tell you when it's right for you."

"I've decided a lot in the last few weeks. I decided to come here, I decided that maybe I do need outside help to find the real me again and I've decided that I still want to be a detective."

"Good, I'm pleased that is how you feel. What changed your mind about your profession?"

He paused before saying, "A chance meeting with a former criminal. He was a boy who was heading down the wrong path, I made sure he wasn't sent to prison and it changed his life. It's strange, I've helped many victims of crime but it was that one criminal that helped me to see how important what I do is."

"The Lord loves a sinner who repents," she replied with a grin. "And what about Tom Russell the person?"

It was Russell's turn to smile. "He's making a reappearance. I've made a decision about that too. I couldn't save the woman I loved however I did save a woman I don't even like, but I came to the conclusion that those things were out of my hands. I didn't kill Karen; it's not my fault she's gone. I decided that she would have understood and that she would want me to move on. The other woman seems set to retreat from even trying to be happier, I looked at her and decided that wasn't the way I wanted to go."

"That's great. Be happy Tom and if you ever need either ear again, you know where they are and He is." She pointed to the ceiling.

Russell shook her hand and said, "Thank you Mairead. You might even make a believer out of me yet."

He walked back down the aisle and out into a crisp autumnal day. He removed his phone from his pocket, dialled, lifted it to his ear and said, "Hi Catriona, it's Tom."

THE END

NOTES ABOUT THE TEXT

The story of Sarah Maitland and Elise Watkins is based upon the famous case of Madeleine Smith, the daughter of a wealthy Glaswegian architect who was charged with poisoning her lover Pierre Emile L'Angelier in 1857. The case was so sensational that it was reported in the Australian newspaper the Sydney Mail. The report of the Elise Watkins trial is based upon that story in the Sydney Mail. The original newspaper report of my Victorian murder is based on another case, the murder of a family in Putney in 1831 which was reported in the Windsor & Eton Express. I owe a debt of gratitude to those long-dead journalists who reported so wonderfully the stories of those shocking crimes.

ABOUT THE AUTHOR

Sinclair Macleod was born and raised in Glasgow. He worked in the railway industry for 23 years, the majority of which were in IT.

A lifelong love of mystery novels, including the classic American detectives of Hammett, Chandler and Ross Macdonald, inspired him to write his first novel, 'The Reluctant Detective' featuring Craig Campbell. There are two further Reluctant Detective novels, 'The Good Girl' and 'The Killer Performer' as well as the short story, The Island Murder.

The Russell and Menzies series developed as a spin off from the original novels. It features Craig's former girlfriend, Detective Inspector Alex Menzies, and her boss Detective Superintendent Tom Russell.

Sinclair lives in Bishopbriggs, just outside his native city with his wife, Kim and daughter, Kirsten.

To help other independent authors publish their work, Kim and Sinclair have created Indie Authors World, a company that offers publishing services and self-publishing courses.

BY THE SAME AUTHOR

The Reluctant Detective series

Book 1 - The Reluctant Detective

"I want you to find who killed my son."

Craig Campbell's quiet life as an insurance investigator is turned upside down when Ann Kilpatrick hires him to find her son's killer. He reluctantly agrees but doesn't believe he can really help.

Before long he is plunged into a world of corruption, deceit and greed. His journey takes him from the underbelly of Glaswegian society to the rural idyll of a millionaire's mansion.

Along the way, a death close to home ensures that he has a personal reason to face the dangers and bring the murderer to justice.

Book 2 - The Good Girl

Craig Campbell leaves his native city to investigate the disappearance of a young woman from St Andrews. Initially, it appears to be a simple case of a girl escaping to start a new life but it soon becomes apparent that there are ominous undertones.

When a woman's body is found on a nearby beach the case takes an even darker turn.

Craig focuses his attention on the seedy world of escorts and their clients. A pimp with a violent history and a number of witnesses with their own secrets to protect block his investigation.

He finally breaks through the wall of lies and discovers a gruesome truth that leads to a dramatic and explosive climax.

Book 3 - The Killer Performer

It should have been Craig Campbell's dream job, working for a rock star who was his boyhood hero. But when the target of his investigation is murdered, Craig is the prime suspect.

Despite the police suspicions, The Reluctant Detective is released and begins his own pursuit of the killer.

His investigations bring him to the attention of a Glaswegian drug lord with a vested interest in the case. Craig's own safety is threatened and he is ready to walk away but as the body count mounts he feels compelled to continue the hunt.

Rival drug gangs, jealous musicians, a disturbed rival and a crazed voice from the past are all possible suspects. Craig must find the killer before the finale of their murderous performance brings the curtain down on another life.

Book 4- The Island Murder (Kindle exclusive)

Craig Campbell is all set for a relaxing weekend break on a Scottish island when he meets a group of motorbike fanatics. They invite him to join them for a drink in a pub but the evening is spent with a fractious group of people with one divisive influence.

When one of them is murdered, Craig begins an investigation that reveals jealousy, greed, scandal and more. Due to a storm the island is isolated from the mainland and with only a special constable for help, he discovers that there is no shortage of suspects. Can he find the killer before the wind and rain relents and the murderer escapes both the island and justice?

The Russell & Menzies series

Book 1 - Soulseeker

Detective Inspector Alex Menzies starts her first day in a new job with a call to the scene of a terrible murder. The body of a young man has been left on a funeral pyre with a hole in the middle of his forehead. The investigation into the bizarre murder is lead by Alex's new boss Detective Superintendent Tom Russell.

A vicious, bigoted racist is the first suspect but within days the city is shocked by the discovery of another mutilated and burned body. The killer's signature is a small cross placed in the victim's hand and the terrifying possibility of the city's first serial killer in over forty years gives the police investigators a challenge that will tax all their skills and combined experience.

The killer continues to find new victims and with each death the case becomes more puzzling and the police more desperate. As fear grips Glasgow, the investigative team must find the Soulseeker before he kills again in his search for the truth about the human soul.

Book 2 - Inheritance

A dismembered body is found in a peaceful loch. The police discover it is Gregg Wright, the son of the leader of one of Glasgow's most notorious criminal organisations. With the realisation, Detective Superintendent Tom Russell and Detective Inspector Alex Menzies dread the prospect of a renewed war between two of the city's most violent gangs.

Tensions rise between the criminal elements as the killer remains free and no one on the streets knows who is responsible. Russell and Menzies look to the victim's son and business acquaintances as possible suspects in a desperate attempt to stop reprisals escalating out of control. Meanwhile their bosses are getting nervous and pile on the pressure to see the case resolved as quickly as possible.

When the victim's wife is found, another possible motive is discovered. Is the case related to organised crime or does the reason lie in something else equally dark? The detectives and their team discover the horrible truth but can they stop the killer committing one final atrocious act?

Book 3 - The Harlequin

On April Fool's Day 1983 a cruel prank goes horribly wrong and a dangerous seed is planted.

Ten years later, a more sinister joke is played and six people die. The Harlequin has arrived. As a young detective constable, Tom Russell becomes embroiled in a hunt that will dog his career.

2003, the Iraq war has just begun and The Harlequin returns with his own 'Shock and Awe' tactic by killing three people in the middle of a Glaswegian spring day. Russell is called once again to pursue the killer.

Easter Monday, 2013 and The Harlequin's finale becomes apparent. Russell is just one of his targets as he kidnaps three more victims and broadcasts to the world a horrifying game show. Can Russell and Alex Menzies finally put an end to the Harlequin's reign of terror?